PseudoPsalms:
Sodom

Peter Adam Salomon

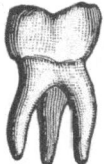

Bizarro Pulp Press
an imprint of JournalStone Publishing

Bizarro Pulp Press books may be ordered through booksellers or by contacting:

Bizarro Pulp Press, a JournalStone imprint
   www.BizarroPulpPress.com

   ISBN: 978-1-945373-72-5

Printed in the United States of America
JournalStone rev. date: March 26, 2017

   Cover Art: Matthew Revert

   Interior Formatting: Lori Michelle
      www.theauthorsalley.com

Advance Praise for PseudoPsalms: Sodom

Peter Salomon's collection of dark poetry, *PseudoPsalms: Sodom*, is nothing less than pointillism in print. He presents individual lines, unconnected by the conventions of punctuation—tight, taut lines that, as each poem nears its conclusion, merge with others to create a matrix of meaning. This is a collection "Where anticipation/Suicides in a scream" and readers must follow the poet as he "dance[s]/In the shadows/Touching innocence/With sharpened claws" . . . and in the end, all is dissolution darkness as

"Suddenly
The way the storm breaks
Leaving poetry
Nothing but broken words
Letters scattered across the paper"

—Michael R. Collings,
WHC Grandmaster of Horror (2016)

Religion, Science, Dreams, Mental Illness, Love, Hatred, Fear, Philosophy—*PseudoPsalms: Sodom* runs the gamut of the emotional and psychological spectrums. From brutally violent and dripping with blood to subtle darkness that tugs at the heartstrings, Peter Adam Salomon delivers poetry that will make you shudder, cry, smile, and—most importantly—reflect on his words and their layers of meaning long after you finish reading this collection. Beautiful and haunting at the same time, *Sodom* is yet another example of Salomon's extreme and delightful expertise in his craft.

—JG Faherty,
Bram Stoker and ITW Thriller award-nominated author of
The Cure, The Burning Time, and *Carnival of Fear.*

*For the dragon
Storm . . .*

Without light there's no shadow

Table of Contents

Writings
Song of Songs
(Song of Salomon)

14ᵗʰ Century Fantasy

He cried
Crystal non-entity tears
Until the machinery jammed
Veins and arteries clogged
With neon plasma in this
14th century world

Technological passion
Alone in rapture
Thrust and torque
In an imitation velvet fist
With artificial intelligence controls
Automated response
And synthetic whispers

Still
Abandoned
In non-reproductive recreation
Where claustrophobic paranoia
Is nothing
More than spilled seeds
In the garden
Of this silken cell

The next concept
Discovers 14th century fantasy
In the new millennium
Of robotic prayer
And synthesized passion
He is
Isolated

With simulated emotion
Left to cry
Crystal non-entity tears
Into an imitation velvet fist

A Child, Lost

Dreams echo
The nightmare

After the trauma
The disorder
Before the cure
The therapy
Within the hope
The despair
Inside a shed
The victim

So lost

A child
Frightened
Alone
Holding to a stranger's hand
Led into shadow
And loss

Screaming questions into silence
Pain drowned in incandescent light
With the touch of a stranger's hand
In the helpless rage of eternal night

The victim
Inside a shed .
The despair
Within the hope
The therapy

Before the cure
The disorder
After the trauma

The nightmare
Echoes the dream

So lost

A stranger
Holding to a child
Leading into shadow

And Answers

Where religion goes to die
       Punish non-believers
       So whispers silence
       In the prayers
       Of atheists
       That all unfairness is a lie

I search for answers
Proudly questioning the truth
The act is not the answer
Neither domination nor submission
Where anticipation
Suicides in a scream
Leaving you bound and blind
As I leave my mark
Upon the most delicate
Of parchment

A tear rages
And ignorance is bliss
The lie eludes me
Preoccupies the thought
       No matter what I convince myself
       The truth is written on your skin

And As Will I

Somnambulistic wanderings
Down a deserted lane
Broken hearts scattered on the pavement
What I thought was truth
Was just a lie

I entertain thoughts of suicide
In the living room of my mind
With wildflower gin
And crudités

Time will pass
Laugh and die
As will you
And as will I

Angstian

Dancing on the ragged edge
Alone together apart from the crowd
Stolen away to shadows

Where the wicked go to be alone
With their evil thoughts
And vicious deeds

Touching the innocent
With sharpened fingers
When lust overshadowed the fear of discovery

Exploring sanctimonious fantasy
With each unbuttoned button
As children begin to cry

Pseudo-religious opportunities
Bless me father
As dogma caresses belief
I dance
In the shadows
Touching innocence
With sharpened claws

Animalistic Imagery

Consummate the passion of anarchistic melodies
In the palaces where witches lie

With the first drawing
Of hands on a clock
The artist created time

      In collections of collectibles
      Converted slayings of prehistoric rituals

One inconsequential human soul
For the worth of a human life

Silent screams (in glass bottles)
Within padded walls (in wine cellars)

Beg for compassion
From a disinterested deity

Animalistic imagery
      Taste the bloody wine
      The body of the Christ child
      Sacrificed to a holy war
      Upon the altar of your soul

Bless The Lord My Soul

My mind
Burns
Flames leap higher
Closing in
With your vicious touch
And violent kisses
Memories of you burn the brightest
Scalding heat between clenched fingers
Around your fragile throat
Praying to an agnostic God
To grant this one simple prayer

Flames lick
Tasting the fuel of you
As poetry burns

Choices

A   Ripping through the air like a beating heart
Torn from living flesh
To feed the innocent

B   Breaking within a moment of ignorance
Antidotes to love lost over the generations
Exorcise the ambiguity from the mystique of emotion

C   So much furious sound without meaning
Psychedelic psychobabble
A violent theory scratches the border of madness
Masking the broken heart within a bleeding hypothesis

D   Memories condemned to die at your touch
Sentenced and executed
Strapped down
Injected with electricity and hydrochloric gin

E   None of the above

Civility

The red velvet curtain divided
Revealing an empty stage
And two ancient actors
Trying to remember their lines:

'Paradise returned,' she whispered,
'But the heavens were diseased.'

'The cure failed,' he said,
'Before the victim died—not after.'

(Exit)

Collection

Strike the band
Close the curtain
Shut the door
Pull the plug
End the poem

Heirs gather round the shroud
Crocodile tears
Fall on purple prose
And yellowed poetry
On fading parchment

Fight the will
And testament
To claim the stolen crown
Pitiful collections of inheritance
When the final word is read

Amen

Contrasts

Different styles of time
Multiple levels of calendars
Balanced by weights and measures
Circular feet in a triangular world
Verbs in contrast with objective nouns
Subjects buried in objectified shrouds
Crowds of people through empty halls
Fighting peaceful intentions
With violent calm

Thy will be done

Creating Light

For the ages
For the night
For wicked pages
For vicious light

I drowned once upon a time
Into a dream
Within your eyes
And all the pristine words
Of all the fading poetry
Could not define our truth

The ages pass
Memories fade
This moment passes
When I held you in my arms
And together
You and I
We created light

Within your eyes
I found the dream we drowned
Grasping
For an unexpected kiss

Deceit

I went to my funeral today
It was a somber, sullen affair
Sparsely attended
Should've been raining
But no
Clear skies
Couple fluffy clouds
Few scraggly mourners
And me
In the box
So they thought
And perhaps I was

I remember dying
Stabbed
I think
Strangled maybe
Bitch fought back
Killed her
I remember
Before dying of the wounds
She left me
Should go to her funeral
That'll teach her
See if anyone's crying for her
No one's crying for me
Not here at least

I visited my grave today
Someone left a flower
Groupies do love their serials

Guess that's me
Not that they loved me while I was alive
Course no one knew
Maybe if I'd been one of the stupid ones
Caught
Imprisoned
Sentenced to die
I'd've had all the groupie love I could handle
Course I'd be behind bars
Limited to horny penpals
And masturbatory fantasies
Like all the others
Too stupid to get away
With murder

Better free to plunder and pillage
I think
Even if love would've been nice
Every so often
But now I'm 'dead'
My crimes splashed across history
And Internet memes
The groupies come out to play
On my grave
Leaving flowers
And panties

After they buried the box
They closed all those cases
Leaving me free to follow groupies home
To collect more flowers
And panties
Of course
So much better than letter writing
Behind bars
I think
I need a new signature
Wouldn't want to be caught

Now that I'm truly free
Safe and home
In those shadows you walk by at night
Watching
Always watching
Waiting
Always waiting
I'm the ghost in the attic
The monster in the closet
The settling of your house
The branch tapping on your window
The dripping faucet
The dog barking at nothing
And I see you
There
Safe
Secure
Behind locks
Alarms
And deadbolts
But no one is safe from me

Diplomacy

The dog was far too big for such a little girl
Well-dressed men placed bets on how long she'd last
While women in sparkling gowns drank sparkling summer wine
Laughing their artificial laughs behind raised glasses
As they waited for the bell to ring

The cage was twelve feet by twelve feet
Rubber-matted
With chain-link fence
Reaching twelve feet up
And when the handler unlocked the door
The dog dragged him in
Snarling
Snorting
And spitting
Lunging toward the little girl
Huddled in the corner
Beneath a tired sheet
She'd tied around herself
Sticking her arms through the holes
And more tears revealed
Ribs
Burns
And those cylindrical bracelets
Of scars
From rubbing against the restraints
Long enough to bleed
Heal
And bleed again

A lovely woman

Hair twisted and swirled into one single blonde curl
Raised a glass
Smiled a smile as fake as the laughter
Made a toast
Downed half a hundred dollars' worth of champagne in a single
blonde sip
And then broke the bottle
On the bell
And the dog crossed half the cage in a single bound

Well-dressed men
Screamed
Bloody screams
Spitting words out
As women in sparkling gowns
Beat against the chain-link
To antagonize the dog
And make it more vicious
Than starvation and beating
Had already done

The little girl
Scrambled up the fence
Dog jumping to bite at her heels
Drawing blood
But failing to get enough of a grip
To pull her down
For the feast

She climbed until hitting the chain-link ceiling
And then gripped
With toes and fingers
To cross to the other side upside down
The dog
Snarling
Snorting
And spitting beneath her
Jumping

And biting the air
With thunderous crashes
Of inch-long teeth

Men tugged at their collars
Sweating
As they screamed
Their blood lust soaring
Beating their chests
To goad the dog
Beating the women
To appease their hunger
As the women beat the fence
Screaming their own bloody screams
Demanding blood
In the cage
To satisfy their desolation
As the dog jumped and jumped
Trying to reach the little girl
Who dangled just out of reach
Clutching the chain-link ceiling
Looking over her shoulder
At the dog jumping and jumping
Until she smiled
Counting the beats between jumps
The moments between screams
Of men and women desperate for entertainment
Starved for blood
And then she let go
Twisting as she fell
In that heartbeat break
As the dog descended from a leap
Trying to bite her leg off
And the women paused to take a breath
To scream louder
And the men pulled back a punch
To hit harder
The next time

The little girl landed
Not behind the dog
But on the dog
Wrapping strips of sheet
Around
And around
His neck
Until she was naked
And the dog was dying beneath her grip

Well-dressed men demanded blood
While women in sparkling gowns gave it to them
But they wanted more
And in order to get more
They needed the little girl
Standing over a dog not yet dead
But close enough for her purposes
So they unlocked the cage
While she wrapped ripped rags around herself
In mockery of sparkling gowns
And then
She smiled
Woke the dog
And followed the blood
Of well-dressed men
And women in sparkling gowns
Out of her cage

Do Not Listen

Remnants of sanity
Pleas of broken hearts
Scattered on the surgical table

We could be together
Until time ends
Or so the ancient poets say
     But enemies of friends
     Do not believe

God watches over me
But refuses to offer aid

I want to hurt
To kill
To taste
To feed the hunger

We cared
I thought
We loved
Or so I believed
And when I asked
Your God replied
     But enemies of friends of mine
     Do not believe
     And took you away
     Before taking away my mind

Sanity left me
Alone to hurt

PseudoPsalms: Sodom

To die
To be your feast
You led it out the door
On a surgical leash
Cutting out my prefrontal cortex

Here I am, they tell me
Living in this hollow shell, they tell me
The voices in my head tell me tell me tell me
Not to listen to these friends these friends these friends of mine

Dream of the Sacrifice

A robed procession
Through the middle of church
Walking blindfolded in a crowd
Hearing their unholy thoughts
As they sing the holy mass

They place my numbed body upon the wood
And leave me as a sacrifice

I start to die

Others before me have been selected
None have lived to spread the tale
For the sovereign good of society

Here I stand
Wondering what all the fear is for
I stare through stained glass
Light touches me
As I die

The others who have been sacrificed surround me
Teach me
Touch me
Love me

We could return
But no one wants to leave

Equality

Famine and death and victory celebrations
Plague and laughter losing the unnoticed war
All the bruised colors upon a rotting corpse
Leaving behind a protesting soul
Crying out to prejudice with open arms
For fairness, vindication, vengeance, and retribution

The generation gap breaks down
Upon the coroner's steel
Scalpel slicing through differences
Between us and them
Beneath the skin
We are all the same

A war was fought
Won and lost
As the casualties went through geometric progressions
Reaching monumental proportions
Partial equality was achieved
Ignored
Because we are on one side
And they are on the other
Even though we are all the same
The wall was built
To keep us in
More than to keep them out

Even Asleep

The glory of your eyes
Even asleep their color inspires
The rain softly shatters against the windowpane
Running as tears
Down crying glass
Fog settles in for the morning
The light reflects
Creating patterns in the prism
Words gently rub against my memory
Circle my mind
And then circle again
Lapping at the sustenance
Paradise brings
Stirring up the past
Remembering the whispers
Shared beneath the thunder
              And the peace
Glowing in your eyes
              The innocence
That breathed your beauty

Even asleep
You smile

I take one last look

        I turn away

As the death bell tolls
Again
Again
And again

Everyone Suffering

Everyone suffering is blessed
Everyone blessed is suffering
We are all alike
We are all the same
We all bleed
And hurt
And laugh
Victim and villain
High and low
Us and them
You and I

There's a little girl
In a cage
In a basement
In Ohio
A married teacher in Maine
Indicted
After her student
Left her pregnant
A priest taking confession
For his own sins
A couple on holiday
In Hawaii
Mugged in an alley
Leaving them with no money
A black eye
A vicious story to tell
A woman in Manhattan
Screaming 'No'
Over and over and over again

With his every thrust
A pre-teen girl
With pigtails
Studying in her room
Caught in the crossfire
Between rival gangs
A cop interrupting a domestic disturbance
Faced with a knife
In the palsied hand of
A drunk husband
A wife forced to forgive
Unwilling to press charges
Despite the split lip
The broken collarbone
And the history of prior calls
A forgotten corpse
Found in a dumpster in South LA
The CSI tech hungover
From when his girlfriend
Broke up with him last night
After catching him with her sister
Who'd left her husband to watch their kids
So she could finally have a break
From twelve hour days
At work
Being hit on by strangers
And bosses
And co-workers
And the old guy at the food truck
They stop at for lunch every day

We all have our soap operas
Our depressions
Aches and pains
Searching for a moment of happiness
Amidst the misery

The couple in Key Largo

Eating breakfast in bed
On day number one
Of their eight day honeymoon
After waiting for marriage
The shy girl in history class
Raising her hand
For the first time
Flush with confidence
After the shy boy in English
Asked her to prom
With a note
Because he was afraid she'd say 'no'
And just as afraid she'd say 'yes'
Which she did
In the hallway
Between periods
In her own note
She handed to him as they passed
The woman going off to college
As the first person in her family
To do so
And following it up with being the first in her family
To graduate college
Med school
Residency at Boston General
And a fellowship at Harvard
Leaving a scholarship in her will
After a career saving lives
And teaching others to save lives
So she could pay forward
The blessings she'd thought unearned
Despite all her hard work
And the love of her family
The young boy recording himself
Singing a song he wrote
About that moment
Right before a first kiss
When you're not quite sure

If she'll kiss you back
Even though she gave you a note
In school saying 'yes'
She'd go to prom with you
And your eyes close
As you lean in
Just a little
Hesitant
Shy
And hopeful most of all
And right before you lean in past the point of no return
You peek
Her eyes are closed
And her lips are open
Partly smiling
And that moment
Right there
He captures it in a song
And it goes viral
Because he kissed her smile

So many blessings
Every single day
You and I
Us and them
We are all the same
Fighting through the misery
To kiss the smile

Everything Negative

As though there is no God
As though I have no soul
I now wonder
What's the use of prayer?

I used to believe in love and God and you—
Now I've lost each belief
In the negative shadows you left behind

Now I've forgotten how to pray
And don't even believe in me

Falling.

Screaming round and round
Falling falling falling down
Waking before I sleep
Even tears have screamed out loud

The sky turned
With the storm of you
Falling
Falling
Falling
Down

Why
Tell me
Why tell
Me
Wait falling falling falling round and round and round
Down onto down into ground going round growing beat
                                         Beat
                              Growing
                    Round
               Going
          Ground
      Into
    Down
Onto
    Down
Why tell me
Tell you why
Screaming   screaming screaming   tear falls down   my
                                    falls down   cheek

PseudoPsalms: Sodom

```
all  down        my
     own         cheek
     o           my
                 cheek . . .
```

Feel the Spirit

The angel stops to speak to us
In religious icon tongues
From the top of the burning tinsel tree
Preaching of victimized children
Like wishes dotting the landscape of memory

Innocent desires fuel our greed
In religious statuary worship cults
Chanting out mass hysteria
As though angels existed

Consumerism becomes commercial prayer
Upon the advertising scriptures
As the angel visits
To warn us
Of the wishes
Of the damned

For One Brief Moment, The Courtyard Burns

Sadistic Christmas elves
Destroy the evidence of innocence

Dreams disintegrate into ashes
With the euthanasia
Of the almost dead

I was never clear on what happened
I held your hand until my world fell to pieces

The devil made me do it in this paradise hell
Nothing is real
It's never what it seems
The courtyard burns
In flames
The heat
Of just one innocent touch

Tinder smokes on the ground
Remnants of a once mighty castle
The land is black

For one moment in time
Burning screams
Crying in the night
For future generations to explore

Legends end
And children scream

My world fell apart when your hand turned to ashes
The courtyard burns
As I throw away the match

Gentle Silent

I answered when they asked
    I believed
    Truth I tell
    And the silent lie

I cared and cried, I told them
Not sure if that was what they waited for
    I searched myself
    Seeking understanding

I answer when you ask
    I believe
    The silent truth
    And the lie I hear

I care and cry, I tell you
Not sure if that's what you want from me
    I search myself
    Understanding nothing
But
    What I wish to do for you
    As gentle as a silent kiss
Discovering insecurities
Vulnerable behind the facade of ambivalence
    I want to believe
    And need to be heard
    They asked
    I answered
    Through understanding's subtle lies

Until I forgot the questions within a gentle silent kiss

He Hath Ordained

Candy-coated killers
Faint at the sight of blood
Like God He hath ordained
Rituals and revelation
For all to believe
The sins a king commits

Candy-coated priests
Forgiving their own crimes
Condemned and damned and left to rot
Where confession is a lie
And holy men the worst offenders
For all to believe
These sins a God commits

Hello

I hoped never to hear your voice again
Despite praying you would call my name
I forgot how empty I could be
How much it hurt to know you

You wish to understand
The lonely thoughts behind the lonely sigh

Poetry is simple
Love is melodrama
When you screamed my name

Patience tries to fill the void
Supply attempts to meet demand
I hear your voice and think the truth
But loneliness denies the sigh

I Said 'No'

I said no
Repeatedly
Out loud
In silence
Screamed
And whispered
Begged
And pleaded
Fought
Scratched
Clawed
I said no
No
And no
Twisting
And fighting
I said no

No

No sound ever louder
Than buttons popping off
My ripping shirt

No

Your hand smelled like fast food grease
And French fries
And tasted of blood
Where I bit my lip
Pressed against my teeth

PseudoPsalms: Sodom

By your palm
To quiet the screams
To muffle the no

I said no
Into the greasy skin of your palm
Trying to bite
Against the pressure
Of limited oxygen through
Stuffed up sinuses
From crying
And the weight of your thumb
Under my nose
While your other hand
Stabbed under my skirt
I said no
Repeatedly
As stars circled my vision
Kicking up and out
To keep my legs together
Slapping your arms
Your face
Clawing
Until you had to remove the hand
Cutting off my breath
Allowing me to scream

No

Twisting
And punching
Fighting
Even as you entered me
To keep you out of me
Off of me
Until you hit me hard enough to bleed
And I twisted away
And you screamed back

41

Peter Adam Salomon

No

But I'd nothing to lose
Now
You'd already won
If rape is a victory
I'm not a prize
You get to claim
I'm a woman
And I have claws

No

I never knew eyes could bleed

You screamed
I fought
Clawed
Scratched
Hard enough to draw blood
Deep enough to draw more

No

My body is mine
Not yours
Never
Yours

No

I
Am
Not
A
Victim

I'll Stay Locked Inside

Magicians and musicians
Practitioners of their illusive arts
Photographs of emotions
Plaster the walls of sanity with elusive hearts

      Staying locked inside my room
      Afraid of my reflection
          The risk
          Of inviting evil in
          When I tried to shut you out

Peeking through the blinds
I see you
In the shadows
Watching me
Watch you

Knowledge eats the ignorant
With a nice Chianti
Of course
Lust arrives with a jaunty wave
An approving smile
Licks its lips
And swallows the pride of you

I throw away the key
     Hide in the darkness
     Watching the world
     And wishing
     Hoping
     For pictures

Of magicians
Locked inside your reflection

Impersonal Rendezvous

The computer spoke of humanity
Flickering past tense graphics on cathode ray flesh
In a world of mechanical antibodies
And imitation cures

Impersonal rendezvous
Merging in artificial moonlight
Surrounded by plastic plants
The computer tried to understand
But failed
As tears rolled down your metal face

Peter Adam Salomon

In Appropriate

I met your husband
He seems nice
Laughed at my jokes
Shared his own
I'm glad he treats you well
And loves you
The way you always deserved to be loved
I'm happy you're happily married
Happier still when you're
Telling me how wonderful he is
With that shy smile
As you unbutton each button
Teasing me with that sweet hesitation
You've long since outgrown
To love us both
And give me treasures and treats
You deny him
And parts of you
He's never known

Today's lesson
Is 'Catcher in the Rye'
She said
That first day
Of class
And he studied
The way the light
Moved through the blinds
Across the room
To fall across her face
And turn those blue eyes

To flame
And all the boys
Paid more attention
In her class
Than the girls
Well, than most of the girls
And some of the boys
But still
She captivated
Stayed after class to help
When asked
And help
Turned to talk
And talking to conversation
And conversations to texting
And texting to late nights
Sharing private thoughts
That turned to private pictures
Shared one too many times
Until the school had no choice but to act
Even if he wanted it just as much as she did

Father offered a helping hand
A gracious blessing
A kind word
To all and everyone
From the aged in the nursing homes
To the newly born
And those in between
Saving special grace
For a boy or two
In that awkward stage
Where grace could be so secret and sweet
A touch or two
Where holy men taught of prophets
And scripture
With wandering hands
And the sound

Of a zipper
Unzipping
Became the only sound
The loudest sound
The final sound

She never meant to tease
It just came so naturally
To stretch
And catch the wind
With hair a little longer
Than it used to be
Over shoulders a little tanner
And curves where planes had been
So very, very recently
And he loved the tease
The watching
Always watching
Waiting to catch her unawares
Even if she always knew
Smiling that secret smile
She saved for him alone
And all the other hims in her life
The old man on the bus
The fat one holding the door for her
The short one watching
While she stretched
Letting her shirt move a little too far north
So the bottom of her training bra
Might be seen
If he looked hard enough
And he always did

She accepted his apology
The way she accepted the blame
If she hadn't made so much noise
Or dropped the plate with dinner on it
Or had cleaned properly

Or done this or not done that
Or done it better
Or not at all
Said the wrong thing
Said the right thing
At the wrong time
Laughed at him
Or didn't laugh with him
Stood too close
Or too far away
Too close to someone else
Or did something she couldn't really name
Or understand
Besides the punch
The slap
The kick
The insult
The curse
Depending on his mood
The number of beers
Or something else entirely
It was her fault
She would tell the ER doctor
Or the police
Or the social worker
Her friends
Family
Tripped down the stairs
Walked into a door
They'd heard it all before
No one believed
But no one did anything to help
Not enough, at least
Besides, she loved him
He loved her
See
He marked her
Made her his

The husband filed for divorce
The teacher was fired
The priest promoted
The little girl molested
The battered wife murdered

Every life is a soap opera
Are you the hero
Or the villain?

(In the election)

(In the news)
A nation thirsts
The famine of the mind
Stagnates the people
Starved for knowledge
Toll the bell for intellect

(In the world)
A nation starves
The famine
Decimates the people
Thirsting for sustenance
Toll the bell for ignorance

(In the realm)
A nation elects
The mind starves for better choices
The people disillusioned
Hungry for salvation
Toll the cursed bell and cast your pointless vote

Inferno

Beneath the waves
Beside Poseidon
Lie the graves
Of evil men
Drowning, reborn, and then
Sentenced to die again

The murderer
With her bloody axe
Chopping
Innocent victims
Serving delicious meals
To ignorant diners
While struggling to carry the corpse from farm to table

The rapist
With his ropes and gag
And all those tools in a plastic bag
Kept in the back of his car
Driving around and around the parking lot
Searching for the weakest chain
Culling the herd
Spreading her legs
While smiling
Pulling hair
Pushing within
Knife against her neck
While cleaning DNA from her skin

The thief
Stealing diamonds

PseudoPsalms: Sodom

Pearls
Rubies and emeralds
Art
Money
And antiquities
Breaking and entering
While rightful owners are left with nothing

The priest
Giving false confession
And deviant communion
In the back room
With little boys
And bored housewives
Leaving sacred vows to wither away
Washed off with a wet napkin
While polluting holy water

The businessman
Cutting corners
Raising prices
Doctoring lab results
Foreclosing on poverty
While cashing in a golden parachute

The politician
Taking bribes
Marinating cigars
In interns
Or eavesdropping on domestic enemies
And covering up the crime
While journalists pretend to care

The poet
Casting accusations of evil
While drowning with the wicked

Insanity Rains

I wake up this morning
No
I woke up this evening

Is it afternoon?
I am not quite sure in this weather
Whether or not weather is
Weathering the storm

Evil disappears in the morning rain
Mourning the death of holy men
With candy-canes and cigarettes

Am I sane or simply pretending?

Insane wanderings down deserted highways
Illusions destroyed by non-existent cars
In this post-apocalyptic world

What lies beyond the borderline?
Over the hills and around the bend
Through the woods
We go
Insanity reigns on reality
And me without my umbrella

Do we dare?

Are we the forgotten frozen victims
Buried beneath our weathered fear?

Inside (II)

The punishment, you see, must fit their crime
Or so the judges have foreseen
The truth is told within a holy book
Pages torn out
Where clergy disagree
With what was written there
By previous generations

Just a stolen kiss upon the silence
When sacrilege came to visit
With a hand upon my knee
The holy man wrote a brand new page
And what was crime
Became sacred
And what was guilt
Became routine

Kneel
Before
Your
God
And
Be
Anointed

Instrumentality

Musicians musicians
Creating passion from obsession
Instrumentality and documentation
Fornicating subterranean rites of passages
In the springtime of our summer years

Released to wander the pathways of imagination
All the verbs performed as nouns
In this fantasy of futuristic tendencies

Developing emotions from subjectivity
Consummation within the delicate masturbation
A bed of roses, a fragile string of pearls
One more failed operation on an unmade bed
Taste the music of a lonely soprano
Before you steal her with a kiss

Is A Sin

The exhausted confusion
Hiding solitude
To memorize immaturity
     Perhaps sanity escaped
     While expectations suicided?
Did reality strike fear within me?
Who is the pawn in this oblivion?

A gentle sigh floated
As the rhyming scream ran down
     Perhaps fantasy is better served untasted

Sound the funeral march
Line the pavements with despair
Design the token interchanges
Only to find that what was once
And is, again
     Within what poets dared to call love
     When they tried to change the meanings
     And failed to grasp the concept
     That love is but a dream
     And dreams have no limits
     No matter what laws might tell you

A sin

In the end
I will promise all that I can lie
Take what is offered
And give what is requested
Deep inside where cynicism hides

And, in conclusion,
This promise is neither as empty as it sounds
Nor as difficult to keep
As though truly I meant to sin

This particular dream
Has no limits
On potential
Or possibility

It Is, Isn't it?

It is
Or so some people say

Insanity teases poetry with the softest taste
Sexuality becomes a hand of solitaire played in padded cells
Walls go up and I tear them down
Who are you?
Do you own a name or does a name own you?
I?
I am
But you already knew that

Quiet
Listen
Can you hear it?
Feel it?
Taste it?
Embrace it?
Take it inside?
Again
Again
And again

> Grains of sand slide through a minute glass
> Constantly flipping it over when I'm empty
> Discharging poetry into you with every thrust

It is
Or so some people say
Isn't it?

Kings and Queens

Into off-world harbors
Imagination draws a blank
On the paper veil of thought
      Mechanized emotions in the frigid temperatures
      As celluloid lovers meet in artificial light

Kings and Queens on plastic thrones
Presiding over cardboard peasants
With the icy mantle of power melting down their royalty
      Confused jesters play the fool
      As one more interdependent death occurs

Last Prayer

In the church of the deranged mind
Created by the neurotic deviant
To stop the thinking
From taking over
These thoughts terrify this white-haired skull
Through the fading gray cells imprisoned within
Fantasies stop to ask directions
Lost in the middle of resurrection
The rebirth of revelation

Return
That which you stole as punishment, tithe, and sacrifice
Demanding compensation
For the stolen kiss

Shining upon my wretched countenance
Waiting for your wrath
To steal my prayer

Medieval History

Did you hear their screams?

Crying into oblivion
When paradise drowned
In quiet moats

A single sigh broke the silence

A touch
So soft upon history
Poetry fades through evolution
          Rune and ruins
          Contemplate the revolution
Future imperfect
As the scream subsides

I heard their prayers
The choir of the damned
Singing holy mass
In fishnet lingerie and bulletproof vests
          Moaning
          Tender nothings
          In the silent whispers of erotica

A touch
So soft upon history
Scholars searching
Discarded artifacts
Of orgiastic consumerism
As ancients sighed
Lies they demanded

Lies they received
When every politician
Told the same damned lies

Castle walls surround me
Torture chamber
Lincoln bedroom rental
Drowning into fantasy
Wearing a stained dress
To work
I scream a whisper
To ignore the touch

Mindless Wanderings

Lost in thought
In a world of non-existent minds
I watch ideals like flies
Swatted by emotional overload
I wait
No
I continue
Wasting time
Within timeless voids of thought
Watching mindless wanderings saunter down country lanes
Thinking thoughts
I think
I've never thought before

Moments in Which

Obsculum Infame
Sprach Jung Frau
Blut Stand Stille

Moments in which
Human nature washed upon the shore
Can you feel the air inside
Or are you dying into day

Original sin as the sexes respond
To the commandments of a useless God
Signifying nothing
The world ends
Can you sense the moment
When the air deflates
And the day is pronounced dead upon arrival

Nerves twitch upon the horrors
The gentle fall of sanity
Softly crossing the line of fantasy
As though the thought had died
Broken upon the sharpened words
Formed from silken caresses
Imaginary séances
Connecting death to love
As the nerves convey the agony
Along the walls of me

(Translation:
Obscene kiss
   The maiden has spoken
   The flow of blood is checked)

Mortal Man

Would you approach, mortal man,
These hallowed halls of marzipan
Where deists flounder to and fro
For fear of living though they grow

And did they speak a name
Of Gods or clowns on Diphthong Lane
When decrepit men share the night
With bleeding claws and vicious light

Mortal man, let your eyes close
To sights beyond your mortal nose
Hear the censure of the blind
And dare to lose your simple mind

In sing-song ignorance, mortal man,
Teach the broken pseudo-plan
Lie down upon your funeral bier
While mortal men cry in their beer

Peter Adam Salomon

No More Rain

The storm continues
Unceasing
This second revelation flood
Missing the ark
To save anyone

The people turn to discarded religions
But fail to believe
Drowning in holy water
And whispered catechisms

There are no animal pairs tonight
No ark to sail the seas
It is too late for prayer
Acid rain
Burned the face of God
For daring to believe

On Job 3:13-14

'Lives without dining,' said I, and closed the eyes
As I listened to political lies
'Eh! He's asleep, and still he sighs'
'Whores offer absolution between their priestly thighs'

'With Kings and counselors,' whispered I
As I went to touch the sky
People sleep and wait to die
People weep and wonder 'Why'

'With Queens and conquerors,' I said
As I searched within my head
People wake in their mourning bed
People wake for the procession of the dead

'With Demons and Gods,' said I
As I tried to steal the sky
People wonder where to cry
People wander, live, and die

' . . . Then had I been at rest, with Kings
And counselors of the earth, which
Built desolate places for themselves.'
Job 3:13—14

Poetess

Within the written word
    A poem

Within the spoken word
    A touch

Gently silent
Violent ecstasy
Biblical sin
Vicious whisper
Touch the poetry

Poetess
Technocrat
Aristocratic tendencies
Vague shadows of generalities
Poet
Empath
Witch

    A sigh
Within the poetry

    A kiss
Within the touch

Witch
Dominatrix
Peasant revolution
Comprehension in the understanding
Submissive

Poetess
Slave

Within the written word
      A poem

Within the spoken word
      A touch

Bow down
And kiss
The poet's ring

Rain Cries Bloody Tears

Blood dew as tears on a rose
To the mourning
Bouquet of you

Confusion preempts sanity
Insane wanderings down desert lanes
Sublime innuendoes prevail
Through a world of deceased beliefs

Neither reasons nor excuses
Love and anger couple in the corner
Solo flights through bleeding fantasy
The rain cries

Afraid to ask
For fear
Of knowing

The edge of madness
Alone in the crowd
Wander down an empty lane
Only to find enemies where friends once were

Rain in the Night

Visions of seers
And mysteries incognito
Or so the writers write
Creating dreams from mundane realities
Or so the poets poet
Mighty warriors
And ancient Goddesses
Line the fabled halls
Midnight dances and fairy tales
Line the tree with Christmas balls

Rain tied in knots
Around the finger of God
Beauty beckons like a beacon in the moonlight
As rays of diffracted sunbeams
Create rainbows in the night

Knowledge causes disbelief
Scholars dream
As sanity sinks in
Sexual innuendoes in the virgin lies of prostitute spies
Misunderstood nuances continue unabated
Visiting a lover's dream in a lonely bed
Mourning dances and fairy tales
Tell such pretty lies
To touch your pretty sighs

Rape the Innocence

Suicide the anger
Sacrifice the embryo
This subtle whisper calls to me
Drains sacred blood from holy flesh
To feed the damned

Kiss your innocence

Rape the weakness
Violate our sanctity
Tie semantics through religion
Share with me this icon touch
And let my soul be saved

Heal your torment

Crucify sanity across violence
With enthusiastic rapture
Kiss vicious compassion
As flames lick sexuality
With a biting gentle laugh

Whisper your sighs

Within the suicide
I taste the holy sacrament
Of baptismal flesh
With demon claws
Screaming your blessed name

Realize your temptation

With a kiss
A torment
A whisper
That it had been your time to die
And mine to bear the pain

Ravings of a False Prophet

Search inside
Within the hidden depths of soul
> Find eternal emptiness
> Then find the key
>> Escape the prison
>> Which masks the fear

Question what you see
> Deity, wholesome, wicked
> Power, life, and death
Ritualistic riddles hide the secrets of eternity
Behind aggressive animosity
Simply to touch forbidden answers

Question if you will
> Choose to open rusty chambers
> Or will you choose sacrilege and sacrifice
> To know the truth they kept from us

Question if you can
> That what is known is known is known
> Rapture, revelation, revenge, and retribution
> Study prohibited knowledge and whisper it to me

Wish to be a God
> Science cannot save you
> Only makes the ovens more efficient
> Religion fails over and over and over again
> To the point that anti-religion

Becomes a religion all its own
Philosophy lies in truth
Good and evil gave birth to sophistry
There are no answers to be found

If you study only what they allow
How much will you never learn?

Reality in Flames

Personified in vibrant colors
Flames in ecstasy
Forked tongues lash out

Strange new worlds at our fingertips
New visions for unseeing eyes
The seer wants a miracle
To bring the mighty out
Fallen soldiers wanting battle
Children needing burial
Believe that all is well
But the fantasy burns
In the corners of reality

Flames consume color
Burning in this human hell
For all the sins we commit

In horror
They laugh as they die
Silent screams of fallen soldiers
Children in makeshift tombs
Cemeteries overrun by holy wars and weaponized disease
The meek shall inherit
An empty world

Remember

The touch collapsed
      The revolution
A smile remembered
      The revelation
As the future prepared
      The retribution

They speak in tongues
Telling their petty lies
Pretty torments destroy simple lives
Holocaustic images
Defeat ignorance
As a smile is prepared

Forget the collapsing touch
As pretty images
Burn pretty lies
The simple torments will be defeated
As long as we remember to prepare

Revolution

An increasing thought
Bright against the subtleties
Of remembrances and false illusions
A battle cry
Then silence
In the ruins of war
The smoke dissipates and disappears
Leaving the hint of carnage
A metallic tinge
Lingering in the heavy air
As a single thought increases
Repeats itself on the lips of the dying
The prayers of the damned
The songs and psalms and soliloquies
The battle cry of revolution
        There
        Is
        No
        God
        But
        Me

Rip the Shadow

Rip the shadow into shreds
Words bite like ice
Little children dream of glory
Marching off to fight the darkness
Holy knights in sacred rites
Teach innocence
On the way to battle
With a stolen kiss
That glory is a lie

Sane Inside Sanity

Ignorant tears
Cascade
Like waterfalls
Over the edge of the world

Sane inside sanity
This troubled soul seeking peace in suicide
We ask questions of ourselves
And we, in turn, pretend to find answers

Mind ripped apart
With electric claws
Breaking hearts
With lost potential

Can I ask
If you exist?

To speak the truth
The truth I need
The need you know
The you I lost

Is there a reason for punishment?
Is there an end?

The pretty pills
So many of them
One by one by one
Until they're gone

Ignorant tears
While pretty pills carry me away
Over the edge of the world

Sanity Reigned

Into what was
Where why became how
And who became you
Watching towering walls fall up
And rise down
With every politician lie
White-padded cells
Past infinity
And future tense

In the drawing room where marble paintings dry
Reality lines the gutter of my mind
     Like senators in the cellar
     Drinking mouthwash
     Out of crystal goblets
     And calling it champagne

All the children lie like dolls in violent apparitions
Smiling similes and metaphors of sanity
Dying like candy canes melting in the artificial sun

Into what once was
Why how became where
And you became who
Here in fairy tales today
White-padded walls contain me
Within insane wanderings

     In a soul I once owned
     Corporate shills bought empty suits
     Repeating platitudes no one believed

Sanity reigned over an empty world
Drunk on mouthwash wine and dollar bills

Screams: In Everyday Reality

Lim f(x) = f(x1)

    In constant usage
        Analytical nonsense
And the screams
    Are always there
Always here
       To remind me of living
Alive if only
    Because I think I hear screams
I think I hear
Breathing until I forget to breathe
Closing the book
    When I scream no more
    When I no longer hear the screams
    When I think
        No longer

(Every)
Scream
    I think I hear
Screams
    (Every) day
       Like

   c
 k   l
r   o
  o c
   w k

Empty mind running in empty circles
Squared numerals
      Beating
           Keeping time only I can hear the screams
Madness falling off the edge of   s
Edge of edge of edge of   a
      You know the reasons   n
      Behind the screams   i
Screams   t
      I think I hear   y

(Every)
      Days go by
Like clockwork
Bright lights brighter lights brightest lights
      Confusion
           Volume lowered with electric shocks to the
cerebellum
        Screams
People hear me
I want
      To leave
          Want
      To scream
          Need
      To die

Mind control
      I do I did I will
Do you understand the want the need the scream
         Now
Talk to me please talk
      Please
      I can scream
Watch me scream
No
Don't watch me look away out the window where the pretty clouds

float
>That one's a turtle
>There a butterfly
>And a clown with an axe chopping down a cherry tree
bleeding bloody sap
>And screaming
>The tree screams
Can't you hear
>The screaming tree?

Down the silken path wandering the silken path on the silken path
with silken paths of silken paths where silken paths lead me down
down down silken paths without you

Like clockwork
>Keeping time with things
>Falling off the edge of the edge of the edge of the world of
the world of the world
>I fall   screams
>You fall   screams
>I feel   screams
>I fell   screams
Wait
>Slow down metal bands biting into my skull
Electricity
>"Clear!"
>NO
Wait   no screams?
>No screams
>No screams
>Screams?
>No screams
Peace?
>No screams
>"Clear!"
NO
>"Clear!"
No screams?

No screams
            Screams?
(Every)
        Days like clockwork
            No screams alone inside my loneliness
Clock stops
                    "Clear!"
            Electricity
    NO
Wait   listen
        I hear no screams
There are no more screams
No screams
Silence
Deep breath
Silence
                    "Clear!"
            Is this peace?
            Is this sanity?
Electricity
Murder   punishmentmurdererpunished
                    "Clear!"
        peace   no screams
    (Every) . . .
    Days of silence of silence of silence

    (Every)
    So often
    I remember your screams
    My axe biting through your neck
    Bright cherry blood dripping like sap
    Again
    Again
    And again
                    "Clear!"

Silent Screams

Time passes
But some things never leave us
Beautiful dreams
Like silent screams
Never leave us

Bloodied hands
    The devil made
Knife drops
    The devil made me
Silent screams
    The devil made me do it

Sanity breaks out
Finger claws
Vicious fangs
Moon is full
Feasting in a prayer to ancient Gods
The devil made me do it

Bloodied limbs
Sacrifice to hell
Knife stabs
Sacrifice to hell
The devil
Silent screams
The devil made me

I wait for sanity
My soul
Sold into slavery

Leashed to you
Knife in hand
Hand on throat
Tendencies of suicide

Bloodied hands
The devil made
Knife drops
The devil made me
Silent screams
The devil made me do it

Some things never leave us

Simplicity of Fantasies: Somnambulistic Mumblings

Into every life
(The challenge is to do more than survive)
In reality
(Through poetry)
Or any life
(And fantasy)

I remember
When love was simple
      Poet
      Hedonist
Classic strangers

(They Meet)

Not trusting
To be the poetry of it all
Afraid of the fall
Mountains seem to move
Or is it the clouds

(They Touch)

Hold together
To ward off the cold

(They Talk)

Forever sorry

For what might have been
Poetry never seems to say it all
Wondering if trust
Is the landing or the fall

(They Touch)

In the heart
Darkness is a dance
        Je t'aime parce que vous etes tu
Hold together
Gaining strength from weakness
Do I trust you
And does it matter

(They Fall)

Hearts entwined
Draining individuality
Somnambulistic mumblings
But all this talk is only poetry
And leads nowhere
Except back to where we were
First scene
Overture stirs the senses

        Wilkommen
        Bienvenue
        Welcome

(They Love)

The acting out of clichéd words
Rehearsed actions
Reciting lines
Like lovers in a mechanized world
Mountains seem to move
Or is it the clouds

PseudoPsalms: Sodom

Could it be the spin of my heart
     Or just the spinning of the world around an axis?

To have you all to myself
Or share with the world
     Would you want to share with me?

(They Fight)

Hedonistic pleasures
Touch that part of me
Let caution to the wind
Shatter the mirror
Violently destroying the reflection
Do I have the strength
To fight
And do I want to
     You know the pain
     You know the hurt
Try to see through my eyes
How I ache when you hold too tight
And whisper your erotic sighs

(They Love)

On the razor line between sane and insane
Reality and fantasy
     I have fallen
     And saved myself
     I will not have that strength again
But simply holding your hedonistic soul
Cannot hope to stem the rising tides of poetry

     How can I expect
     You
     To save me
          When you are the one
          Pushing me over the edge

(They Lie)

The poet wants to touch
The hidden secret heart of you
No one else has touched
      All this talk is only poetry
      One more dying society

Can I break your mirror
      Blood drips down
      Screams in agony
      Each time you taste forbidden fruit
      From forbidden trees
      Seduced by temptation
      To taste the poetry
      Of crescendo

(They End)

      Au bientot

(Epilogue)

I fought the pretty reflections
All the different yous of you
Hedonistic souls drowned in the simplest of fantasies

(Finis)

Sodom

Don't look
Little girl
Don't turn around
Nothing to see
Little girl
Keep your eyes closed
Your head down
And run
Little girl

Don't look back
God will protect you
If you obey
Little girl
There's nothing to see
Just run
Don't open your eyes
You don't want to know
Little girl
How the guilty suffer
Little girl
The sinners
Burning
The evil
Punished for their crimes
Little girl
Damned to hell
Where angels fear to tread

Don't turn around
Little girl

Run
Little girl
Eyes closed
Head down
And run
Don't look back
Little girl
Don't ever look back
There's nothing to see
In the shadows behind you
Just keep your eyes closed
Little girl
I'll let you go
I promise
Little girl
You have my word
Just don't turn around
Little girl
Keep your eyes closed
It's almost over
Little girl
Almost
There
Little girl

Such pretty eyes
Little girl
I told you not to look
Ordered you not to turn around
But you had to be defiant
Had to look
To see
Little girl
You just had to know
What I looked like
And now you're not only a victim
You've become a witness
Little girl

Can't have that
Little girl
You shouldn't have looked
Little girl
Should have kept your eyes closed
And God would have protected you
I would have let you go
Rather than turn you
Into nothing
But the dried paths
Of salty tears
Down the cheeks
Of those who buried you
Little girl

Startled Eyes

The birth of poets
Told me once
That suicide was the answer
I asked of them:
        'What was the question?'

Startled eyes were silent
Tender hands with slender fingers
Shook and clenched into a gentle fist
They stared at me
And wondered who I was
To question them
These ghosts of genius
        'Artistry beyond what humanity pretends to create.'

Startled eyes shattered silence
As I wondered all the reasons
If solely to prove I belonged
Gentle hands shook and clenched
As I questioned all their answers
If only to convince myself to write

Still and Quiet

Hearts spoke truth
Into the vast divide
A whisper bridged the distance
And the echo shared the sigh
All was still and quiet
Because the truth is love
Most whole when it is pure

Storm of Deity

For the devil
Will take those
Who cause harm
To the loneliness
Word
The loneliest prayer
On lonely nights
Alone again

Endless
Array
Of
Arrhythmic
Syllables

Piety
Consummated
With
Sacrilege
Birthing
Religion
With a lonely word

Storm
Convicting
Deity
To
Disbelief

Pitiful God
Believing we believe

The lies
Of prophecy
The prophets lied
Each time the prophet died

Strong Under Everything

Love, lost lonely alone among the memories
Where shame and emptiness came to life
As imaginary playmates in the cloistered neighborhood
Where every cobblestone and weathered antique left you lonelier
than you should ever be
And the beauty of innocence suffered the ignorance in the quiet
Lost lonely alone seeking imagination, crescendo, and escape
Until so little remained of the innocent to curse or cure or
comprehend
Though beauty never faded, you withered within where compassion
hid
Waiting for the sun, for nourishment, for salvation
Of your own design, no need for anyone else to save you
A flower growing strong surrounded by vicious weeds with cruel
thorns and crueler words always tearing at the velvet fabric, the
silken skin, the pale sweet flesh to get to the beating, beating,
beating heart of you
Surviving and thriving, growing and feasting on the life you always
should have led and deserved and imagined and lived
Among the weeds, stronger than you ever knew, glorious and
glorious, brilliant and brilliant, wondrous and wondrous
Leaving shame behind in the ashes where it belonged
Just a memory, its own emptiness, knowing you shine brighter than
the sun, a flower, strong and sure, and beautiful beyond words

Subtitles

The scene of the crime
Flashes on a silver screen
Screams of panic predominate
Questions asked
And answers given
Without thought
Just another fantasy
Scattered on the table
Battle scars reign
Searching for motives

Massing in places of commerce
Masonic temples shadow reality

Movie subtitles in a foreign language
We cannot hope to understand

Sweet Dreams, Love

"Sweet dreams, love," said Daddy
Then he knelt and looked under the bed
"No monsters there"
Before checking the closet
"No monsters here."
He turned out the light,
Shut the door,
Slid home the bolt,
And latched the chain

Ashley opened her eyes
Blinked once or twice
Huddled in the blankets
She peeked over the sheets
Holding tight to her pillow
As the shadows surrounded her
Closer
Just a little closer
And closer still
So many shadows
Close enough to reach out
Touch
Caress
Claw their way into the pale moonlight
Filtering through the only window
The bars shadowed in long grey stripes across the floor
As Ashley blinked
Huddled
Peeked
Holding tight to her pillow
Until it, too, surrounded her

PseudoPsalms: Sodom

Closer
So very close

To scream, she'd have to open her mouth
But she'd learned long ago
The shadows and the pillow
Were only waiting for her to cry,
To open her mouth
And invite them in

So, in silence, Ashley blinked, huddled, peeked
As the shadows surrounded her
Burrowing inside with claws and bars and pillows
Until nothing remained but darkness
Silence
Loneliness

Ashley blinked
Huddled
Peeked
And smiled
Flexing her claws
Baring her fangs
Waiting under the blankets
Beneath the bed
In the closet
For Daddy to return

Originally published in HWA Horror Poetry Showcase Volume III, 2016

Take the Time

Has anyone ever stopped
Taken the time to be
Alone within the crowd
A tiny smile
Melting into sugar tears
When understanding eluded me

And so we pretend
Or play at delusion
Until the smile melts

Has anyone ever stopped
Asked or answered
About the emotional overload
Which occurred
When the smile died

And so I watch
From somewhere
Far away
Where the crowds
Cannot touch me
And the wicked smile
Burns into confusion

And all the questions
Lied within the truth somewhere
All the words are simply words
When every melting smile
Stops to wonder why

Teach the Agony

The fist tightens upon the world
Landing within the factories
Where children work to death
To make toys for children
They'll never be able to afford to play with
One more agony defined
Lost amidst the multiplicity of agonies

Child soldiers
Child brides
Child slaves
And child laborers
There's a pattern
If you look
Are you looking?
Do you see?
Or do you turn aside
To focus on petty microagressions
Because a pronoun is a pronoun is a pronoun
Is vital and important and worthy of your protest
But a seven-year-old girl
Stoned to death
On the other side of the world
For the crime of being raped
You can ignore
From the safety of your ivory tower

Searching to try
Trying to understand
Through religion's eyes
Where God has failed

To protect the child within us all
I searched for divinity
And found hypocrisy
As you ranted and raged
The insignificance of your elitist battle cry
Should shame you
When so many need your help
And you refuse to see

The Glow

There was only you in every dream
Only you in all the poetry I knew
There was this glow surrounding us
Lighting up your eyes
So much joy in just a name
Happiness in just a touch
Love within the poetry

There is this dream that never ends
My name lingers on your lips
So pure and red and mine
Your touch echoes on my skin
Gentle, tender, and complete

And in that perfect moment
When all is said and done
When the words are silent
And the poetry a touch
I will kiss those lips so red
So pure and you and mine
And in the gentle, tender dream
The glow surrounds us both
With glory I never deserved

Peter Adam Salomon

The Last Man

There's not much time left now
Machinery breaking down
Individual parts failing
A lung there
A heart valve or two
Circuitry and electrical conduits
Not so much overloaded
As simply aging out of service
One by one

Corroded cables
Frayed matrices
Held together for years
Decades
Centuries
With duct tape
Spit and prayer
Each repair
Using obsolete refurbished parts
Scavenged from salvage
Where available
And jury-rigged from odds and ends
Found in scrap heaps and rusted piles
Left at the side of the road
Or shoveled into ancient landfills
When this model was new
Or newer at least

Now, few original parts
Are in original working order
Rather all have been replaced

PseudoPsalms: Sodom

At one time or another
With artificial replacements
Some printed out on faulty printers
And others simply hammered into place
When they wouldn't fit properly

Still, I've survived this long
On various machines
Pumping blood through leaky veins
And air into punctured lungs
Small patches glued on
To keep the air mostly inside

The digestive system was the first to go
Dying off a while ago
When the last supply of imitation intestine
Spoiled when the medical bay died
IV tubing feeds nutrients now
Into the few inches of skin
Remaining of my flesh
Until more tubes
Take the waste away

Little more now
Than a brain attached to an old battery
That once powered a machine
Alleged to be transportation of some kind

Every so often my heart beats
It's the third
I think
Maybe the fourth
Not human
Nor artificial
The last artificial heart broke down
So long ago
I barely remember the pain
Of the myocardial infarction anymore

And human hearts wore out long before that
Dog, I think
The med bay thought the sutures wouldn't hold
Didn't believe the anti-immune suppressants would work
But they have
So far
Even if the heart beats oddly
Barking at me in the middle of the night
Not that this night has ever ended
Since the sun's been missing in action
Even longer than the humans
I used to know
When I was human
Or, at least, more human than not
Or more human than whatever I am now

I've a mouth
For what little good it does
No food to eat
No throat to swallow
Even if I could find any
Not that I'm mobile
Stuck in this chair
So long I'm now a part of it
Or it's a part of me
Not that I've spoken
Not in so long
I'm not sure I remember how
There's no manual
With instructions on how to breathe
Fill the lungs
With enough air to use tongue and jaw positions
To form sounds
That sound like words
There's no one to talk to
Nothing to say

But now I'm dying

PseudoPsalms: Sodom

Finally
I lost my hands sometime in the distant past
So it's not like I could kill myself
Instead I've just been waiting
For enough individual parts to die
Or, please God, for the battery to give up
Despite massive built-in redundancies
And the built to last wind turbines
Recharging the battery every time
It begins to drain

I'm dying now
I can feel it
I lust for it
Not that I remember lust
As anything more than an esoteric thought process
The wanting remains
To fade
To end
To die

I remember talking
Once, when there was still hope
Someone might hear me
Rescue me
Save me
Instead, in some cruel twist of fate
Laughing at me all these years
And decades
And centuries
I've had no choice but to listen
Since even after every other part of me has failed
My ears still work
I made one transmission
Never knowing it would be
My last transmission
As my body began to fail
And that

Peter Adam Salomon

By cruel mistake
I'd leave
The transmission on internal repeat
For all these years
Decades
Centuries

'I don't want to die'

Echoing in the dark
Repeating until the components fail
And now
If I have to hear those words one more time
I swear I'd kill myself
But I just don't know how

The Lie

War
Wicked soldiers
On the battlefield
Screams of anger pierce the dark
Death's Dante dance
Biting through love's question mark
The law of imagery
Shattered in poetic moonlight
The pen ripping through paper flesh
As semantics fail to die

A hundred thousand hundreds
Falling into disrepair
Hearts afraid to beat
And bodies afraid to live

Walking through silhouettes
As images on mirrors shadow
Waking up to die
To wonder about reality
To fantasize and cry
The wicked soldiers
Toys in a child's mind
To love and lose and love again

What the poet searches for
Is near impossible to truly find

The Whore Prayed

The whore prayed
The priest sinned
The angel fell
The devil rose
The light created shadows of darkness
The dark made the light brighter
Within the beating heart of death
A thousand lives were lost
Giving rise
To charity
And sin
Compassion
And lust

On her knees
Ripped fishnet stockings
Against the pavement
In the middle of the street
Hands clasped in prayer
The whore caressed rosary beads
Dressed in cheap lingerie
And cheaper perfume
To hide the stench
Of rotting teeth
And wicked infection
As she prayed

On his knees
Perfectly creased pants
Against the thick carpeting
In the nave off the altar

PseudoPsalms: Sodom

Hands clasped around her
The priest caressed everyone in reach
Dressed in a three-piece suit
And fine cologne
To mask the stains
Left by spilled offerings
And wicked lipstick
As he sinned

Banished from heaven
For sins a God commits
The fallen angel
Rules in hell
Damned to eternity
In the wilderness

On wings of flame
And wicked anger
Demons fight gravity
To reach heaven
Escape damnation
In paradise above

There's a light
Within us all
A darkness, as well
We're shadows
You and I
Nothing more
Nor less
Than shadows

Evil in the deity
And goodness in the devil
Where the heart of the storm
Is calm
The calmest heart is born
In the compassion of lust
And the charity of sin

Theme

Leave reality behind
To sing realistic songs
Quoting journalistic pretensions
      Enter the imagination
      Aromatic colors
Fantasy choirs sing vision songs
Caress the idea
Pleasure palace slavery
My leash around your precious neck
Submit
Submit
Submit

Time

Only time can tell
Walking the avenues
Down the pathways of my mind
In a funeral gown on your wedding pyre
As though the breaking heart was dead
'. . . You should not have to pay
For love
With bones
And flesh . . . '

As though lies are truth
Looking at all the pretty views
Down the pathways of my mind
Walking the avenues
Only time can tell
Such pretty lies
The fire tells

To Dream the Muse

Along forgotten pathways
Where light became dark
In myriad lies in pyramid shape
As the touch became touches
On your paper flesh

I watched the liquid smoke
Curl around the figment of imagination
That once described you

I dream you once again
Alone with a touch
Prisoners of passion
And the warden of obsession
To dream the muse
In poetry creation
Where the touch
Curled around you
And wrote the world

Tone

She said goodbye
In that final tone
He'd heard before

The first was grade school
When he chased on playgrounds
Pulling pigtails
Before running away
Then junior high
Snapping bra straps
And lighting fireworks
At frogs
In the creek
Behind the old man's rusted Buick
Every so often he'd hit one
And laugh
As it hopped
Into the water
As though drunk
But really it was injured
And wouldn't reappear
After slipping into the water
To escape the noise
And light
Of each miniature explosion
Then high school
When cheerleader fueled jocks
Cornered him under the bleachers
Warning him to stay away
From the girls
They claimed as property

With letter jackets
And used condom wrappers late Friday night
Taking out the frustration of defeat
On compliant mostly-drunk high school girls
Who probably wanted to say 'no'
Until it was too late
For anything but 'yes'
Closing their eyes
To pretend the pain away
Like their friends told them
It'd be over soon enough
And they'd get to keep the jacket

He kept a list
Of each girl who said goodbye
Every time he heard that tone
Saw that look
In their cornflower eyes
Part disdain
A little pity
Mostly disgust
Finally
One day
Almost done with high school
There was that teacher
Who put him in his place
When she caught him looking down her blouse
She shouldn't have worn that shirt
With the loose collar
Or the sheer silver bra
With lace edging
She talked to him
Filled with righteous indignation
In that tone
After class
Until he stood up
Towering over her
And for a moment

The briefest instance
Her voice faltered
The tone changed
Shifted
And disdain
For just a second
Was tinged with something that might almost be called fear
He responded
His body responded
His heart
Beating quicker
Hotter
Harder
At that tinge of fear

It took him a while
To understand
His response to her
And why
But then
Months later
He understood
Remembering the swell of her beneath that sheer silver lace edged
bra
He didn't climax until remembering her shift of tone
The fear
Her fear
Pushed him over the edge
Sent him searching for more
It became his quest
The holy grail
He'd never known he was seeking
Epiphany
In her fear

She said goodbye
In that final tone
He'd heard before

So often
Over the years
Since high school had taught him so much
He'd returned
This night
To thank his favorite teacher
She didn't understand
When she answered the door
Why he was holding her bra
In his hand
Offering it to her
'I cleaned it,' he said, 'for you'
But she backed up
Said 'goodbye'
In that tone
Before slamming the door in his face

He shrugged
Unlocked the door
With her key
Smiled
Then waited for her tone to change
To fear

Unusual

Unusual
And satanic dreams
Visions of horror and other terrors
Friends and fiends lie in wait
For evil to behave

What was never
Is now
In these
Unusual and satiric dreams
Of mine

Visions of beauty and other reflections
In a nondescript world
I tried to behave
And failed

Voyeur

He watches from the shadows
Hidden by windowpane glare
And curtains
Even the tree outside
Where he peeks through leaves
Studying her
Relaxing in bed
Watching black and white movies
Dressed for sleeping
A little chilled
He knows
As she pulls Beatles socks
Up over painted toes
He'd watched her paint
Through the window
In the living room
Just the other night

The wind brushes branches
Against the window frame
Scratching
And she looks up
At the sound
Breaking into the movie
And then laughs
A little
At herself
For being scared
And skittish
All alone
Dressed for bed

In her Beatles socks
With a plate of cookies
Fresh from the oven
Warm
On a chilly night
Drinking hot chocolate
As another breeze
Brushes branches against the window
And she looks
Again
At her reflection in the glass
And he looks back
Smiling at her
From the shadows
Where he watches

Remembering
The way she walked
And smiled
When he followed
Too closely
That first day he saw her
He smelled
Lavender and vanilla
Every so often
A hint of rose
Fresh from flowers
Not perfume

And, now, he smiles
Watching her
As she laughs at herself
For being scared
Before biting into another cookie
Dipped in hot chocolate
Watching an old movie
Alone
Even as he watches with her

Whispering her name
With the breeze
Brushing against the window
And he calls it a date
Third this week
Just the two of them
Once more
Watching old black and white movies
And wanting nothing
But to knock on her door
Say 'hello'
If he had the courage
To leave the shadows
For her

Safer just to watch
Keeping her safe
Watching over her
Sharing a movie or two
Until she falls asleep
And he can sneak inside
Finish the still warm hot chocolate
And taste the cookies she baked
Pull the blanket up
A little higher
Because it's chilly
In her bedroom
Watching her sleep
Wondering if she's dreaming
Of anything interesting
Perhaps
In her dreams
She knows he's there
Keeping her safe
Watching over her
Sharing a movie or two
He reaches a hand out
Almost close enough to brush the hair off her face

But not quite that close
Close enough to feel her breath
On his fingers
And no closer
When a breeze
Brushes a branch
Against the window
He jumps back in fright
And almost laughs at himself
But doesn't make a sound
Finishes one cookie
Savoring each bite
And then
From across the room
Blows her a goodnight kiss
Before fleeing
To the safety of the shadows
Watching over her
Keeping her safe
Until dawn
When
Once again
She watches him disappear
Back into her favorite dream

What You Wanted

Ravenous need
Enthusiastic want
The right lover
At the wrong time
Too hard to let go
Too soft to lose
Is it too little now
Or too much then?

You just never knew
Might never know
What you wanted
Needed
Loved
Lost

When Did and Why

When did and why
Who, what, and where
        Subtlety too subtle for the simplistic mind to comprehend
        Earth is just the point
At the bottom
Of a galactic question mark
And life is simply a wait for the final answer

Where It Started

Where it started with a smile
Wondering
The beauty beyond
The beauty of you
Deeper than beauty
      Did you understand
      When it was, exactly,
      Where aesthetics met semantics
      With a kiss in the darkness
The welcome dream
Ends with a vicious tear
Following the smile into loneliness
To wonder
The smile beyond
      To divine divinity within
      Could you make me understand?

White Padded Cell

Mind wanders into darkened corners
    Sleep comes easy to tired eyes

Listen to speeches in this dual-personality world
Two people share my soul
Share my soul
Share my soul
Political thoughts on diseased personages
Debating percentages of unused pregnancies

No order to meaningless
Syllables
Of love
In empty voids
Of vacuum

Intellect conquers poetry
We do not know the language

Enclitic minds of psychoprophylaxis

Tired
Thoughts of
Pregnant cis-gendered males
Tired patients
As
My mind travels
Exotic worlds
Lush
Tropical dreams

Hold me back

White padded walls
Close down around

Tie me down
Restrain me
White walls fall down
And I drown
In the desert
Of you

Wind

the violence beyond compassion

You

You died
They taught
For sins
And shrouds
Time and again
Nailed to a tree
A pole
A cross
You died
Again
And again
With every sin
Real or imagined
You died
So that arrogant men
In suits
With matching ties
Could rule in your name
Because
You died

When prayer failed
Religion turned aside
And now blessed hypocrites
Corrupt children
Asking for details
Of private moments behind locked bathroom doors
Old men with palsied hands
In their own pockets
As they ask their sacrilegious questions
And offer absolution

For thirty silver pieces
And a touch
Just there
For a moment
It'll be ok
No one needs to know
Maybe a kiss
It'll be our little secret
Have some candy
It'll wash the taste out of your mouth
Besides
He died
For your sins
Don't say a word
Until the next time
When empty men
Ask illicit questions
Of children experimenting
Or wives struggling to find themselves
As they're told being lost is meaningless
The men in suits
With their hands in their pockets
Know what's best
Knowing nothing else
Insisting they've the answers
When they're not even listening to the questions
Until there's nowhere
For struggling wives to go
But back to where they were lost
Told by arrogant men
It's your fault
No one else to blame
Obey your husband
Your church
Like when you were just a girl
Telling us of private moments
For our own enjoyment
No one needs to know

It'll be our little secret
No one cares about your questions
We weren't listening
Have some candy
It'll wash the taste out of your mouth
Besides
He died
For your sins

Damn the platitudes and piety
Pull the nails out
No matter how great the pain
Spread your wings
Blaze your own trail
And leave the past behind

Song of Songs (Song of Salomon)

The Song of Songs, also known as the Song of Solomon, Canticles, or the Canticles of Canticles is part of the Writings, the last section of the Hebrew Bible (the fifth book of Wisdom in the Old Testament of the Christian Bible). It is revered for its 'celebration of sexual love' dealing with two lovers 'praising each other, yearning for each other, proffering invitations to enjoy.'

This unique Biblical exploration of love and sex has always fascinated me.

In this Song of Songs/Song of Salomon, I've taken my own personal exploration. Mainly, what happens *after* such a monumental love story?

In the Song of Solomon, the reader follows one relationship from meeting to courtship to consummation.

Now, in my own Song of Salomon, follow along for their breakup.

Storm (a haiku)

Your song of thunder
The beauty of my lightning
Poems of our storm

Breathtaking

Rage against the breathtaking storm
Try to hold to the lightning
At least capture the rain
Escaping through my fingers
Drowning into soft clouds
And whispered thunder
To find you
Drowning beside me
The storm
Whispered
Screaming your name
The rain
Slipped free
No matter how we raged

I Dreamt the Kiss

I dreamt the kiss
Or wanted to
Needed to dream
A specific dream
Long ago
And every moment since
Remembering what never happened
But did

Where the dream
Began with the taste
Of gin on your lips
A breath of wildflowers
So far away
So close
When a dream
I never dreamed
Ended with
That one fragile kiss

Chained to each other
Bound
Drowning
And grasping
For a dream
Starving
Thirsty
For a gin-soaked kiss
I'll never know
Nothing but a dream
Dreaming

Every dream
I've ever known
Ending in a kiss
Unexpected and oh, so welcome

What Was I Thinking?

To think every precious thought
What was I dreaming?
Hoping?
Expecting?
Random thoughts and possibilities
Misted into moonlight
Darkness
And shadows
Like every thought
I'd ever dared to think

Knowing you hurt
Hurts
When there's so much still to know
I'll never know
Of the delicate
Fragile
Storm
Of you

The Someday Kiss

In the twilight world
We created together
Where light meets dark
We explored together
Shadows in the rain
We danced together
To symphonies of thunder
We drowned together
Waiting for the promise of a kiss
We dreamed together

Lingers

Your voice whispers
Words I've yet to read
And the whisper
Lingers
So much more than words
There's something secret
In the depths of your eyes
Doesn't everyone see it
Hear it
Know it
In your whisper
Your words
For me alone
And everyone else
But there's that secret
It lingers
I swear it lingers
Every single day
Every time I see your name
Read your words
The smile
In the picture
You shared for me
And me alone
So much alone
Always alone
This lingering loneliness
Sharing your words
With the world
For me alone
I know

You're alone too
Surrounded by so many
And still so far away
Lonely
Secret
In the depth of us
When there's never been an us
That's the secret
Alone
Waiting
Hoping
It lingers

Our Word

Some words fight back
Claw not to be said
Or beg to be voiced
Innocent words shade evil
Hiding in the shadows
Where light fears to dwell

Some words
Haunt the empty spaces
Where innocence dared
To smile
And ignorance damned
To weep

Words fail
Grasping for something
Anything
Everything
To say
Chained to a memory
Of what potential
Might possibly have been
If only
Someday
Were today
Rather than yesterday
And gone
Before ever beginning

And still the words claw to be said
So I spoke and once said

The words meant the world and nothing
Like any words
And all words
And no words
In the silence between words
Where each breath matches
Each beat matches
Each touch matches
Lingering
And haunting
Alone
Again
Again
And again
Until the last word claws free
The goodbye word
Begging to be voiced
Lingering
Drowning
In the emptiness

There is a language to poetry
Of words
And silence
And all the moments
Unlived
Unshared
Unknown
In a momentary fantasy
Of a different life completely
Of possibility
And potential

So I know the word
The only word
The last word
Our word
Clawing and begging

PseudoPsalms: Sodom

I close my eyes
Take a deep breath
And turn reality
With a whisper
Through goodbye
And love
Through potential
And desire
Through possibilities
And hope
Into the word
The only word
The last word
Our word

And in the silence
Of us
I
Make
A
Wish

Exorcism

I'll try to be honest here
Wondering why I miss you so much
So many questions still to ask
Too many answers still to share
Gone
Just like that
And in abandonment
I try to find myself
Without you
And it hurts

That's the true honesty
That makes letting you go so devastating
I can't find the words
They slip away
Lost in the storm
And I wonder what I'm supposed to do now
When all I want to do is talk to you
Listen to you
Watch you
Kiss you
What have you done to me
With all this leaving
With the push and pull of us
It's been longer now apart
Than together
And never fully together
You slipped away
Before I ever held you
In every return you took over more of my heart
And broke more of me

Every time you left
Until only pieces of poetry remained
So I write
To get the passion onto paper
Out of me
Exorcising you
Even though it's far too late
I'm already damned
I've always been damned
And the angel I fell in love with
Kissed me goodbye
Without a kiss

Broken

I'm tired of writing poetry
Something broke inside
And I don't know how to fix it
Or even know what part of me is broken this time
I'm empty and shadowy
With random moments of pity
And anger
Because I know what's missing
I know me
This will pass
I'll say
But it's a lie
I tell myself
The same lies
I always tell
But I remember every hurt
Every stupid thing I've ever done
Or said
Or barely survived
I save the hurts
And they become words
And poetry
But the hurt's always there
It never fades
It never goes away
As fresh this moment
As the moment you said goodbye
Again

Something broke
And I wonder
Are you broken too?

Wanting nothing more than to be able to ask
Fearing nothing more than knowing
You're whole
Complete
Without me

Moving

Moving on
I'm trying
Then I remember
What I'm leaving behind
And shake with the emptiness of it all
How do you regret doing the right thing?
Where do you go from there?
When you'd do it all over again
Embrace the pain of it
The sorrow
The hollow breath
Of missing you
Because there was nothing else I could do
Every time you asked me to let you go
When you couldn't leave me
And I never wanted you to leave
I never wanted to say goodbye
And never did
It hurt too much
That word
And I know
I think
That you've moved on
I hope you have
I hope you're happy
I need you happy

I'd do it again
Again
And again
Regretting it

Every single time
Ripping my own heart in two
To protect yours
And hating myself for doing so
When there's nothing else I can do
When you ask anything of me

Peter Adam Salomon

The Storm of You

There's poetry in the storm of you
Born of light
Creating shadows
In the subtle darkness
Just as there's a precious piece of you
Left within me
Long after goodbye
So there's a part of me
In you

Even in a perfect world
There's so much distance
Anxiety
Pierced against us
So many reasons why not
Until a wish
Defies all reason
Knowing there's no hope
No happy ending
No kiss at the end of an unexpected dream

Somehow we live in a magical world
We've created
Out of poetry
Where all the reasons
Piercing the bubble surrounding us
Fail to destroy the wish

So we live with the sorrow
Hoping for a different answer
To a simple question
Of what the future holds

There's poetry in the storm of you
Written in wind and rain
Thunder and lightning
And all I ever want to do
Is read you

Peter Adam Salomon

Walking A Dream

The walk was just a walk
Through a canyon
Along rocky coastlines
Up mountains
On a path in the forest
Beneath a canopy of leaves
In soft rain
And sunny skies
Thunder and lightning
Bringing the storm
Around us

It started with the softest touch
A brush of shoulder
Against shoulder
A smile
And then

Yes, what happens then?

The dream ends
Or begins
Fingers intertwine
Arms swing with every step
The motion soothing
Soft
Gentle
The rhythm of the walk
Melodies and harmonies
Feeling your palm against mine
Your fingers soft

Gentle
Where we touch
And then

Yes, what happens then?

The dream ended
Began
And the rain falls
The sun shines
The clouds send shadows
Dancing around us
Our arms fall still
In a clearing of our own creation
The softest
Gentlest
Pressure
And suddenly we're face to face
Your hands in mine
Fingers locked
The pulse quickening
Beneath your
Soft
Gentle
Skin
Thunder shocks
Makes us jump
A little closer
Close enough to feel the breath of you
Melting into my own
And then

Yes, what happens then?

You're a dream
And every ending
Leads to a different beginning
And then

And then
And then
The soft
Gentle
Love of you
For you
With you
Letting you go
Fingers releasing their grip
Long enough
To walk forest pathways
Canyon valleys
Rocky coastlines
Up your arms
Over the heart of you
Worn on your skin
Along the pulse
On the side of your neck
Behind your ears
Fingers intertwined
With your hair
Softly
Gently
Pulling you closer
Until I realize
You'll never be close enough
In any dream
And then

Yes, what happens then?

There's a line
Between friendship
And us
This dream we've discovered
Passed it long ago
And it began
Once upon a time

As all dreams do
With an unexpected
Welcome
Soft
Gentle
Kiss
And then

Yes, what happens then?

The dream of you
Continues
Your lips
So soft
Gentle
Smiling
The sun breaking through the clouds
The rain
Symphonies of thunder
We kiss
And kiss
And kiss
Exploring
Learning
Discovering
The taste of you
Finally
Someday
Now
Today
This moment
And the next
And the one after that
Until nothing exists but the kiss
Hearts beating as one
Loud
Out of control
Thundering to drown the storm
And then

Yes, what happens then?

The dream
So much more than just a dream
The spaghetti strap of your tank top
Slides off your shoulder
With little effort
Of my finger
Hooked around the
Soft
Gentle
Fabric
Only to discover
As it slides down your arms
There's another underneath
And another
One after the other
So many layers hiding you away
From me
And even when the last of them
Puddles in a pile
At our feet
Your
Soft
Gentle
Skin is yet another layer of you
Hiding you away from me
While I explore the heart
And heat
Of you
Softly
Gently
With every trailing kiss
From your lips
To the tip of your nose
Your earlobes
Down your neck

Kissing the mad pulse of you
The faint white line
Where the spaghetti strap
Protected your
Soft
Gentle
Skin from the sun
And further down
Kissing your heartbeat
Feeling the life of you
Beneath my lips
And then

Yes, what happens then?

This is a dream
The dream
The only dream
The feel of your skin
Warm and welcoming
Unexpected softness
Waiting to be touched
Soft
Gentle
Where wonder
And woman meet
Beneath covers
And layers
Removed one by one
To taste the heart of you
To feel the heat of you
To be welcomed inside
Home
Soft
Gentle
And then

Yes, what happens then?

Peter Adam Salomon

This is a dream
Nothing but a dream
We're far too far apart
With no hope of being together
Any time soon
And in the dream
There's no ending
No beginning
Only poetry
And hunger
Love and
Soft
Gentle
Kisses
And then

Yes, what happens then?

There's no dream
Remaining
Nothing but this vicious
Emptiness
To be honest
I'm writing this naked
Hungry
Raw
Exposed
With no layers protecting me
From the sun
The rain
The canyon
Forest
Mountain
Nothing between you and I
But skin
Hiding us away
And then

Yes, what happens then?

The soft
Gentle
Dream
Kiss
Of you
And the heat
The passion
The need
The want
Burning
And dying
Over and over again
Every time you leave
Taking more of me
Until little remains
But sad
And empty
Memories
Of what never was
And could have been glorious
Might have been precious
May have been astonishing
So much more than just a wish
This
Soft
Gentle
Memory of a kiss
That never happened
And then

Yes, what happens then?

I'm left
Naked
Alone

Hungry
Dreaming of
A walk
The brush of shoulder
Against shoulder
A smile
In the rain
And a kiss
That never
Ever ends
In the
Soft
Gentle
You
Of
You

Still Dreaming

I just woke up
With your name on my lips
Dreaming of you
Aching for you
Wanting you to see me
Touch me
Taste me
Inhale me
Into the softness of you
With your superpower
Softness
Again
Again
And again

Exploring every inch of you
The curves of you
The wrinkles and the smoothness
The warmth and the wet of you
Those places burned from the kiss of the sun
Those places hidden from the eyes of the world
Finally exposed to me
Given to me
With such ravenous need
Want
Love
Kissing you
Taking you
Giving you
Down the swirls of you
And finally into the depths of you

Where I come home
Inside you
Again
Again
And again

Watching you explore
Watching you fly above me
Watching you return to me
Until we're one
Heart to heart
Beat to beat
The fall of your hair
Around your delicate face
Against my skin
With each kiss
Each rhythm
The harmonies
Melodies
Symphonies
Of joy
Need
Love
Whispering your name
Screaming your name
With each pulse within you
One heart
One final motion
And then

I kiss every delicious inch of you
Again
Again
And again

Our Storm

There's a storm
Down the road
In the distance
Closer than it appears
Over the horizon
The day after
The day after tomorrow

I listen to the brilliant fury of it
The beautiful song of it
Even from so far away
Even after all this time
It reminds me of you
With the wind
Calling your name
And the prayer of you
On my lips

I watch the dark clouds
Dancing
Sharp rays of the sun
Breaking through every so often
A subtle reminder
Of the beauty waiting
After the beauty of the storm
Lightning kisses the sky
Flashes of brilliance
Exposing the world
Washed clean
Beneath the rain
Whispering your name

In the thunder
In the wind
In the electric touch
Of that first and only kiss
We never shared
Except in the dream
Of a storm

Wondering

'How are you?' he wanted to know
But wasn't allowed to ask
Waiting to hear
Needing
Wanting to know
The not knowing
If she's all right
If she's happy
Safe
Calm
Content
That not knowing, it's a hollow hurt
An emptiness
In her shape
In his empty heart
Where she remains
A part of him
Hoping she is
Happy
Praying
Really
With all he has
With every breath and beat and being of him
He wishes to know
She's happy
Hoping she's perhaps maybe a little sad
Without him
With him
The other him
The right him
He knows

He's the wrong him
But wishes
Oh, he wishes
So much he wishes
But the first wish
The one wish
The biggest wish
Is that she's happy
He needs her happy
Needs her to be her
The best of her
And there's so much to her
The glory of her
The sweetness and brilliance and flight of her
Freedom and strength and wonder of her
The wander, too
She wanders
One with nature
Home there
As though a part of nature
She is, he thinks, the heart of nature
She's the sunrise no one sees
And the canyon paths no one knows
Most of all she's the storm
Wild and free and electric
Fresh and powerful and glorious
And for a moment in time
Far too short and forever
She was his
He was hers

'How are you?' he asks
And in the silence
He wonders
Hopes
Prays
Dreams
Her happy

Remind Me

The rain
Reminds me of you
The wind
The sun
The sky
Reminds me
The breath
The sigh
The smile
Reminds me
The sudden twinge
Remembering
The surge
The rush
To share
And then
Remembering
Another breath
Another
Each sigh
Reminds me
But the rain
Most of all
The sound
Each drop
One
By
One
Reminds me
The waves of it
Washing down the window

Reminds me
Every beat
Every dream
Every moment
Reminds me
I lost you
And the rain
Continues
Reminding me
Every day
Reminds me
Of you

I Hurt

No
Seriously hurt
Deep deep inside
Where I never go
Never admit to
I hurt down there
In the darkness
And it's draining
All the light
Life
Energy
Into the pit of me

It's silly
And insignificant
There's really no possible reality
Where that someday kiss comes true
The laughter of the fates
Deafens
But damn it to hell
There was something special
I know there was
I know
Because I hurt
Even in the face of laughing fates
The silliness
And insignificance

I looked inside myself
And hated what I saw
The self-pity

Self-doubt
Selfishness
Even in the selflessness
Letting you go
Broke something in me
I never knew was there
And it's not healing
It's breaking more
Every moment
And I can't fix it
I can't even find it
The hurt is so damn deep inside
Swallowing me whole
Into a darkness
So unlike the dark
I've always known
This is bleak
Not sexy
Hollow
Not muse
Empty
Not poetry
It's fucking dark
I'm alone
No one is coming to save me
And I'm not sure I can save myself

I'm not even sure I want to

Longer

Now it's been a week
Seven days
One hundred sixty-eight miserable hours or so
The sharpness still hits
But mostly I'm numb
Knowing what I've lost
That's the hardest part
The knowing
It's too difficult to focus
Too hard to ignore
This new reality without you
Knowing you're moving on
You've moved on
You're somewhere else now
Over me
Or maybe pretending to be
Over me
Which ends at the same place
Without each other
Alone
And I miss you
So much
Looking at your pictures
A thousand times a day
Without even realizing
I'm doing it
Watching you sing
Listening to you sing
Wondering if you're singing for me
To me
Reading your poems

Until they're memorized
And then reading them again
Wondering if there are new ones to read
I'll never read
Hoping you're reading mine
Wanting you to read the new ones
I've written just for you
Knowing I can't just share them with you
Can't
Won't
Shouldn't
But want to
With all I am
I want to
Reach out
Talk to you
With you
Walk with you
Touch you
Kiss you
Tell you I love you
Because telling you I love you
Might be the truest thing I've ever said
And I've no idea how I got here
How I found you
How you fell for me
How I let you go
Despite never wanting to let you go
You were a dream
Far too short
And I'm not sure I'll ever wake up
And stop loving you
I need to
I know I need to
You're not in love with me
Any longer
And it hurts
To know you loved me

And chose not to
Any longer

Empathy

I whispered you
And you heard
Somehow
The energy of me
Piercing the distance
I hope you feel this
My heart
Bursting
Into pieces
For you
Every moment
I believe in hope
Before remembering
You took hope with you
When you left
When I let you go
Should I have fought for you?
Should I have kept hurting you
In order to keep you?
What choice was that
You left me with?
You're right
You killed me
Each time
And maybe it would help me
To hate you for it
For breaking me
But I can't
I won't
I could never
Hate you

Might be easier
On me
I suppose
If I could stop loving you
Move on
Somehow
But then I remember you
When everything
Reminds me of you
And I fall in love with you
All over again

I Wish I Knew

I wish I knew how to hate you
I wish so many things
But hating you?
I don't know how to do that
It would erase the hurt
Ease the hurt
Wouldn't it?
Would it?
I don't know any longer
I don't know anything
I'm so lost
With these brief moments of finding myself
Lost in you
And then losing myself again

I wish I knew
How to stop loving you
I'm addicted to you
And I need my fix
You feed the muses
Fueling every thought
Into poetry
And I disappear a little more
With each word
And I wish so much
But I'm tired of poetry
And wishing
And hoping you'll find me
When I'm so damn lost
And all the wishing
And hoping

In the world
Doesn't amount to much of anything
But still
I can't hate you
Why can't I hate you?
I need to know
I don't know how
And the most truly frightening thing
Of all
Is that I think
You're teaching me

Just Me

It's just me here
Alone
In the quiet shadows
The moon through the trees
Outside the window
Providing just enough light
To see the empty side of the bed
Where you should be
If you wanted
While you're on the other side of the country
With the same moon shining down
Creating quiet shadows
Just for you

Your name
Whispered into the silence
As I close my eyes
And see you
Fill the emptiness next to me
Feel you
Fill the emptiness within
I see you
I whisper your name
Breaking the silence
With the magic of you
The soft wonder
And the wonderful softness
Creating quiet
Just for me

It's just me here
Alone
Believing
There's a moon
Outside
Through the trees
Waiting for us
To believe
Creating
Just for us

Peter Adam Salomon

She Laughed

I suppose
I made her laugh
And her laughter
Lit the world
With explosions
Of silver
And stardust
Sparkling in a dream
Touched with her laughter
Because
I suppose
I made her laugh
And it was
The sweetest sound
The birds chirping
Snow White and Cinderella
All wrapped up in her
Whistling
A happy tune
With nature
And birds
And laughter
Ending in a smile
To break hearts
So much sacred
And divine
In her laughter
So much holy
In her smile
And
As sweet as all else

She smiled
I suppose
For me
And in the laughter
The smile
The unbridled sacred joy
I found healing
Hope
Happiness
Because she laughed for me
Smiled with me
Loved me

And in her
I found the other half of me
And
Most of all
The glory
Of God's most precious creation
All because
She laughs

Life is

All those new words wait
In the new worlds
You'll discover as you soar
To skies
To storms
To dreams
Of the other side of mountains
Lightning
Thunder
Rain
And maybe
Every so often
Me

An accident of falling
And I caught you
Fought your fear with you
Tasted your happiness
Shared your guilt
Cherished your sweetness
Drowned in your sorrow
Ached for you
Escaped with you to the all of us
So you could breathe
To be good
Always
Your best at being good
Is better than most
And best of all
Your good is
Good

PseudoPsalms: Sodom

Life is scary
You see that now
No God will save you
Maybe one will
But you don't know that God
And you suspect she is you

Life is beautiful
To feel love
Inside your soul
Inside your body
To connect
To someone
To all things
To breathe it in
Like the God you have yet to know

Life is truth
You are Eve
Sticky fingers
Sticky lips
A pile of cores at your bare feet
Your hands on your naked body
Because you are not ashamed
Yet kicked out of one Eden
After another
Because the old Edens no longer fit
Around your arms
Your breasts
Your wings

Exposing your raw new self
You have to leave
When all you want to do
Is lay with yourself in the soft grass
Picking apples from the bending boughs
And breathing in
The knowledge of God

Peter Adam Salomon

Life is glorious
Discovering new words
Exploring yourself
Touching the sky
Flying into storms
Breathing fire
Rising from the ashes
Uncovered
Naked
Pure
Raw
You are the other side of the mountain
The truth
The scary
The beautiful

Life is
You

Raw

Hungry
Aching
Need
I want
You know I want
We both know
You want too
I know you want
Need
Hunger
Ache
I feel it
Even as we deny
All those hungry desires
And floods
Of want and need and aching
There's a secret or two
In the silences
Between us
In the sighs
The private moments
And held breaths
The shaking
Heated touch
Of silver sparkles
Surrounding you
Every inch of you
Caressing
And kissing you
With fireworks
Your laughter

Turns to sighs
And then something softer
Whispered into a kiss
As we fit together
Like a jigsaw puzzle
Finally whole
And we're home
Free
Connected
In the softness
Of us
Where want
Need and hunger
Aching together
Become one
Alone
Alone
And alone

That's the curse
To all our wishes
So I try not to think of you
Those moments
When I want
Hunger
Need
And ache
Until you become my only thought
Your name on my lips
You on me
Drowning
In silver sparkles
I dance with you
While dancing by myself
Trying not to think of you
And thinking of you
With every lonely touch
I think of you

Hoping you can feel me wanting you
Until explosions of silver sparkles
Drown you
In the flood of me

I think of you
And think of you
Thinking of me
As you dance by yourself
With every lonely touch
I want you
Thinking of me
My name on your lips
Me on you
Until explosions of silver sparkles
Drown me
In the flood of you
And we
Become
One

In A Drawer

In a drawer
In a dresser
In a room
In an apartment
In a city
In a dream
There's poetry
A song or two
French lavender and honey
So it smells like you
Your journal
Filled with freedom
Flight
And
Every so often
Me
There are the secrets
You shared
And those you never had the time
To share
But would have
One day
While it rained outside
The window
Of the apartment
In a city
In a dream
And you curled up
With me
In our own world
Where there's

A drawer
In a dresser
In a room
In an apartment
In a city
In a dream
Filled with poetry
A song or two
French lavender and honey
So it smells like you
And I love it there
With you
Here
With you
Always
With you
Until saying goodbye
And saying goodbye
And saying goodbye again
I could fight for you
And would
But I can't
So I won't
I shouldn't
It wouldn't be right
To hurt you
Every day
Loving you
Every day
Making you happy
Every day
And still tearing you in half
Simply by loving you
And being loved by you
So I say goodbye
Again
Always

You're worth fighting for
Never doubt
Even as I choose not to fight for you
That you're worth fighting for
There's so much of me
That wants to fight
To rage
And scream
With all the fury
Of letting you go
Fight for you
For us
To keep you in my life
In my heart
To stay in your dreams
Rather than in a drawer

I keep letting you go
It's killing me
Piece by piece
Harder than anything I've ever done
Harder than I ever imagined

I've realized
After trying to look inside
The way you do so easily
That I've never loved like this
And just perhaps
Never been loved like this
If I thought
For a moment
An instant
A million seconds
There was a reality
Where loving you
Doesn't break your heart
Every single day
While making you happy

PseudoPsalms: Sodom

All the same
I'd listen to that part of me
And I'd fight
And rage
And scream
With all the fury
Of all the poetry
Of all the storms

But we don't live in 'our' world
We live in the world of them
And distance
And what could have been

And we could have been great
I think so
At least

All that's making letting you go so hard
Is the simple fact
I never want to let you go

But I need to
For you
Because I can't keep hurting you
By loving you
By being loved by you
And I know you love me
And it's a beautiful love
Because it's yours
Ours
I'm so stupidly in love with you
And so I let you go
Again
Always

It will forever be our drawer
In your dresser

In your apartment
In your city
In your dream
Our poetry
A song or two
French lavender and honey
So it smells like you

Always
Always
And always

Jagged

Breaking up has so many sharp jagged edges
Memories hurt
And possibilities
Potential
Could have been
Might be
Maybe
Breathing hurts
At the beginning
Everything stings
Cuts
Sharp and unforgiving
And facing the jagged edges alone
Is dangerous
Painful
Lonely
And
I know
I'll never heal
Whole
The way I was
Before
You said 'Goodbye'

Space

They shared a bed
In a dream
With space between
Like ships crossing an ocean
They met in the middle
Only to touch
Briefly
In a dream
With so much space between
An ocean
Of distance
And more
Separating them
Tearing them apart
While keeping them together

Struggling to find herself
She pushes him away
Pulls him closer
Runs away
Returns
So much more than distance
In a dream
With space between
He waits
Lets her go
Watches her leave
Walks her onto the ship
For her to find herself without him
So maybe someday
She'll find her way back

So much more than distance
In a dream
With space between
To find each other
On the opposite side of the bed

Dreamed

She dressed in shadows
Cloaked in storm
And rain
Wind-swept hair
Lightning eyes
She smiled
In the dream
He dared to dream

She sang in whispers
Laughed in song
And story
Creating poetry
With hope, a wish,
And a smile
In the dream
He shared with her

She found herself
In the quiet
Discovering the world
As the world discovered her
Dressed in storm
And rain
Wind-swept hair
Singing in whispers
Of poetry
And smiling
Laughing
In the dream
He dreamed for her

Alive

In the shadows
I touched the softness
The warmth
And welcome
Of you
Hidden beneath protective layers
Like a maze
To find your heart
Covered
Banked
And yearning to breathe fire
Like a dragon
Exploring a strange new land
Filled with lakes to skim
Dipping a claw into the water
Testing the temperature
Before diving
Breaking the surface
In the sheer joy of flight
Free
Unchained
And alive
Alive
Alive
With the beat of independence

Filled with mountains to climb
Each step opening to new views
Scenery never seen before
Never known
Never tasted

Never embraced
And the higher the dragon climbs
The bigger the view
The greater the joy
The truer the truth
In the sheer joy of conquest
Discovery
Exploration
Sensation
Raw
And alive
Alive
Alive
With the rhythm of freedom

Filled with canyons to walk
Oceans to sail
Storms to fly into
And home, most of all
In the beating
Alive
Alive
Alive
Heart of you
Where the soft magic
Sings
Soft
Gentle
Songs
And
Hard
Biting
Songs
And
Soft
Biting
Songs
And

Hard
Gentle
Songs
And everything in between
And more
Where the magic of you
Embraces the complexities of you

The naked joy of freedom
As the dragon
Finally
Spreads her wings
And
Flies

Roar

She's difficult to describe
But I'll try
She is so much more than poetry

She is stolen apples
Snow white owls
Steel rivets
Storms
And dragons
Freedom
And flight
Still so much more
Than all of the above

She is inspiration
Imagination
And innuendo
The tease
And the promise
Hope
Dream
And fantasy

Long walks
Crawling for autumnal acorns
Energy
Symbols
And healing
Mysteries
Magic
And honesty

All wrapped up
In silken hand-sewn bows
With that particular flair
She captures so well
Determined to let nothing stand in her way
To fly
To soar
To be the best of souls
To be herself
To roar
To the heavens
'I am me'
And let the angels fear

Breaking

I broke again
Fragile
Balanced
Barely
On a razor's edge
The blade slicing into me
Every time I breathe
Each time I move
Every thought of you
That blade slices deeper
The pain bites
Deeper
Until nothing remains
But the breaking
Leaking blood
As the blade slices through
And I fall
Again
Left screaming in impotent rage
Cursing
Trying to find myself
To hold onto something
Anything
When you took everything away
Abandoning me
Even though I begged you not to
Told you how much it would hurt
You left anyway

I tried to be strong
But I'm not

I tried to be happy
But I can't
I tried to move on
But I haven't
I tried to keep my balance
But I fell
Again
Slicing deeper
Until nothing remains
But the blade
The blood
And the breaking

Watching

Every moment lingers
The soft sweet breath
You breathed into me
Heated fire breathing dragon
Spreading your wings
Encompassing me
With your warmth

Every moment
Each one of them
And gone
In an instant
Breaking your chains
Our hearts
Soaring into storms
Until nothing remains but rain
Glistening starlight
Watching you fly
Away

Waiting longer than someday
Always
For your return

Magic

Wishes don't come true
Nor dreams
Fantasies
Or mystic spells
There's no potion
Wand
Nose twitch
Mind trick
Or hypnotic watch
Only lonely time
Passing
Until the sting numbs itself
And leaves behind
Echoes and shadows
Of what might have been

So, numb, I continue on
Lonely time
Passing
Trying to figure out
What magic could fix us
When we did our own breaking

No More Psalms

I'm trying not to hate you
For hurting me
But it's not easy
None of this is easy
But even knowing it isn't any easier for you
Doesn't help
Just adds to the hurting
Knowing you did this to us
And the final straw
The swift sudden goodbye
You forced on me

There was found
Something special
Sacrificed to your fears
And I'm trying
But I hurt
Abandoned to the nth degree
Because you dared to love me

I know all the rationales
The reasons
The necessities
But nothing changes the empty hollowness
The spikes of anger
The pit of this
In the heart of me

I hope to hell this is helping you
But I've no idea if it is
No way to tell

You took that away from me
The ability to know you're ok
That's what you took
So all I can do is hope
You're better now
Without me
Than you were
With me

Waiting for Fury

One moment at a time
That's all I know
Each moment
Every one of them
Stings and pierces
Slings
Arrows
Every cliche
Repeating
Ad nauseam
Until little remains
But disillusion
And I'm tired
Of being disillusioned
Of being tired
Of waiting for fury
To strike me down
For daring to tread
Where angels
Fear

Past Tense

There was a dream
But morning came
And the dream dissolved
As dreams do

There was a dream
Wrestling with an angel
To climb a ladder to heaven
Where seven stalks
And seven ears
Changed the world
Until an Eden dream ended
The world moved on
Uncaring
Of the dreams
We dared to dream

There was a dream
Where the man you loved
Returned
But the dream
Ended
Because 'was'
Replaced 'am'
When you said
'The man I was in love with'
the dream dissolved
as dreams do

There was a dream
Heaven sent

Or hell
Begun with a kiss
'Hello'
Only after we said 'goodbye'
The dream dissolved
As dreams do
Because you woke up
While I sleep on
Dreaming
Still
Of the woman I love

Ends

And alone, it ends
Suddenly
The way the storm breaks
Leaving poetry
Nothing but broken words
Letters scattered across the paper
Without meaning
Or purpose

Alone
Even poetry
Ends

About the Author

Peter Adam Salomon is a member of the Society of Children's Book Writers and Illustrators, the Horror Writers Association, the Science Fiction & Fantasy Writers of America, the Science Fiction Poetry Association, the International Thriller Writers, and The Authors Guild and is represented by the Erin Murphy Literary Agency.

His debut novel, *Henry Franks*, was published by Flux in 2012. His second novel, *All Those Broken Angels*, published by Flux in 2014, was nominated for the Bram Stoker Award for Superior Achievement in Young Adult fiction. Both novels have been named a 'Book All Young Georgians Should Read' by The Georgia Center For The Book.

His short fiction has appeared in the Demonic Visions series among other anthologies, and he was the featured author for *Gothic Blue Book III: The Graveyard Edition*. He was also selected as one of the Gentlemen of Horror for 2014.

His poem 'Electricity and Language and Me' appeared on BBC Radio 6 performed by The Radiophonic Workshop . Eldritch Press published his first collection of poetry, *Prophets*, and his second and third poetry collections, *PseudoPsalms: Saints v. Sinners* and *PseudoPsalms: Sodom*, were published by Bizarro Pulp Press. In addition, he was the Editor for the first books of poetry released by the Horror Writers Association: *Horror Poetry Showcase Volumes I and II*.

He served as a Judge for the 2006 Savannah Children's Book Festival Young Writer's Contest and for the Royal Palm Literary Awards of the Florida Writers Association. He was also a Judge for the first two Horror Poetry Showcases of the Horror Writers Association and has served as Chair on multiple Juries for the Bram Stoker Awards.

Peter Adam Salomon lives in Naples, FL with his wife Anna and their three sons: André Logan, Joshua Kyle and Adin Jeremy.

Boiled Americans by Michael Allen Rose

Boiled Americans is a puzzle box in book form, inspired by the violence of living in urban America and exploding the tendency to forget or ignore.

Great American Slasher by David C. Hayes

Baseball, apple pie . . . and murder.

The Bohemian Guide to Monogamy by Andrew Armacost

Here, a strange labyrinth of interlinked short fiction assembles itself into a darkly moving novella that deftly explores the bottomless pain and pleasure of love and commitment, the hinterland between youth and adulthood.

Surreal Worlds edited by Sean Leonard

An anthology of surrealistic compositions created by some of the finest names in genre fiction. A showcase of international talent undaunted by the conventions of language and common narrative structures. Here is timelessness. Here is Surreal Worlds

How to Succesfully Kidnap Strangers by Max Booth III

Do not respond to bad reviews. If you must respond to bad reviews, please do not kidnap the reviewer.

ADHD Vampire by Matthew Vaughn

He came, he conquered, he was distracted a lot

Notes from the Guts of a Hippo by Grant Wamack

A rugged journalist travels to Brazil in search of a missing hippo researcher and the notes left behind lead to something earth shatteringly revelatory.

All Art is Junk by R. A. Harris

Lana Rivers, a girl with paintbrush hair, is missing and it's up to Lancelot, her cyborg knight, and his bionic conjoined twin, Cilia, to find her before her evil father, a disrespected artist turned mad-scientist, performs a terrible experiment on her.

Cherub by David C. Hayes

Cherub wasn't like the other boys—too slow, too rough— but he didn't deserve what that hospital did to him, and now he will make them pay.

Skinners by Adam Millard

Los Angeles, the City of Angels. At least, that's what the brochure says. What it fails to mention is the earthquakes. Oh, and the flesh-eating creatures lying dormant beneath the concrete, waiting for the chance to surface once again. Their wait is over . . .

The After-Life Story of Pork Knuckles Malone by MP Johnson

What's a farm boy to do when his pet pig becomes an evil, decaying hunk of ham with slime-spewing psychic powers?

A Lightbulb's Lament by Grant Wamack

A gentleman with a lightbulb for head wakes up in a world full of darkness, hooks up with a beautiful ex-prostitute, and an old man who can heal people; he travels down south to find the mysterious Creator.

The Horror Show by Vincenzo Bilof

A poetry novel—a narcoleptic, amnesiac Nobel Prize-winning poet becomes the subject of an experiment to cure madness.

Beyond by Jordan Krall

From Jerusalem to Mars, psychiatry and the unraveling of the universe

Gravity Comics Massacre
by Vincenzo Bilof

An absolutely shitty novella involving comic books, aliens, a serial killer, teenagers in an abandoned town, horror-trope dream sequences, and an ending you're going to hate.

Glue by Scott Lange

Sticky bowels and sticky situations.

Ascent by Matthew Bialer

Is the 8 foot tall creature haunting a small town in Iowa in the fall of the year 1903 the product of a hoax and collective imagination or was it one of the first documented paranormal event in America? This epic poem grapples with these questions.

Elusive Plato by Rhys Hughes

The last in a long decadent line of piratical Spanish eccentrics, Bartleby Cadiz grows up in isolation to be as mad, bad and metaphysical as his ancestors. But he feels there is something different about him. What can it be?

The Fairy Princess of Trains
by Christopher Boyle

Danny's mediocre life turns upside-down when his couch starts whispering to him. Then he's charged with a supernatural mission: Rescue the Fairy Princess of Trains.

Terence, Mephisto & Viscera Eyes
by Chris Kelso

9 new science fiction stories from Chris Kelso

Industrial Carpet Drag by Bruce Taylor

Chemicals make you do great things!

Bizarro Bizarro: An Anthology

The finest bizarro short stories from 2013.

Necrosaurus Rex by Nicolas Day

Necrosaurus Rex tells the tale of Martin, a simple janitor, who takes an unfortunate trip through time, becomes a violent mutant, and the father of us all. There's 14 billion years crushed inside these pages, and most of them are pretty nasty.

Day of the Milkman by S. T. Cartledge

In a world dominated by the milk industry, only one milkman survives after a terrible storm sinks all the ships and throws the Great White Sea out of balance.

Moosejaw Frontier by Chris Kelso

An unapologetic disaster of metafiction

The Boy Who Loved Death by Hal Duncan

From blackest humour to bleakest horror, with twisted relish, Hal Duncan's eighteen tales dig into death—and the life that goes with it.

X's for Eyes by Laird Barron

Between the machinations of the disciples of black gods and good old corporate skullduggery, it's winding up to be of a hell of a summer vacation for the Tooms Brothers.

Omega Grey by Seb Doubinsky

When professor Todd Bailer embarked on a psychedelics quest to discover if the land of the Dead really existed, he had no idea he would threaten the cosmic balance of the universe by triggering a real-estate conquest of the new Frontier.

Berzerkoids by MP Johnson

The first short story collection from Wonderland Book Award-winning author MP Johnson

Retch by David Bernstein

What would you do if you were cursed to puke right before you reached orgasm? You'd do anything, right? (You know you would.) Find out what one wealthy, good-looking, playboy will do to try to end his abhorrent curse.

Static/Orgone by Jamie Grefe

A double-novella of literary grindhouse nightmares and theoretical post-apocalyptic vengeance.

Wonder Weavers by Matthew Bialer

An epic poem about a mysterious sighting in 1896.

Battering the Stem by Bob Freville

A darkly comic urban crime novella. What would it take to make you beg?

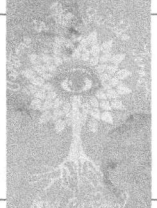

Cartoons in the Suicide Forest by Leza Cantoral

When we're dead
You know she'll adore us